Staffordshire Library and Information Services
Please return or renew by the last date shown

Hednesford _PE_

2 8 AUG 2018

3 OCT 2018

23 OCT 2018

. 3 JAN 2020

WITHDRAWN

'My brother is full of the virtues of your Lyrebird Lake.'

Tammy lifted her chin high and stared into his eyes, as if suspicious of his tone and the implication that he might disparage her home town. Her irises were a startling blue, and reminded him of the glorious sea on the Amalfi Coast—disturbingly attractive, yet with little waves of tempest not quite concealed and a danger that could not be underestimated. He knew all about that.

She went on in that confident voice of hers, that managed to raise the dominant side of him like hairs on his neck. 'Lyrebird Lake has everything I need,' she stated, almost in a dare for him to contradict.

He bit back the bitter laugh he felt churn in his chest. A fortunate woman. 'To have everything you want is a rarity. You are to be congratulated. Even if it seems a little unrealistic for such a young woman with no husband.'

Tammy smiled between gritted teeth. This man had created havoc in her usual calm state since the first moment she'd seen him. Too tall, too darkly handsome, with sensually heavy features—and so arrogant, so sure of his international power.

One more dance and she was done. No more being nice to Leonardo Bonmarito.

Mills & Boon® Medical™ Romance
is proud to return to Lyrebird Lake!

Fiona McArthur brings you a fresh instalment
from her fabulous mini-series…

LYREBIRD LAKE MATERNITY

Every day brings a miracle…

It's time for these midwives
to become mothers themselves!

**Previously we met Montana, Misty,
Mia and Emma**

*'Thank you, Ms McArthur,
for a thoroughly enjoyable time spent
in your world of Lyrebird Lake,
and I can't wait to read of your many more
delightful characters too.'*
—Cataromance.com

Now it's time to introduce Tammy…

**You'll love her as much as everyone else
in Lyrebird Lake!**

MIDWIFE, MOTHER... ITALIAN'S WIFE

BY
FIONA McARTHUR

First published in Great Britain 2011
by Mills & Boon,
an imprint of Harlequin (UK) Limited,
Large Print edition 2011
Eton House, 18-24 Paradise Road,
Richmond, Surrey TW9 1SR

© Fiona McArthur 2011

ISBN: 978 0 263 21755 1

Printed and bound in Great Britain
by CPI Antony Rowe, Chippenham, Wiltshire

Dear Reader

Tammy was never going to be anyone's wife. Wife meant 'love for ever', and she didn't believe in for ever, and then there was that 'obey' word. She'd always had issues with authority. Plus she had her son—the only man she needed in her life.

Then she met Leonardo Bonmarito—tall, gorgeous, a brooding Italian doctor who was never going to settle in Lyrebird Lake, and who would never allow her the freedom she thrived on. And his son placed her own in danger. So what was she doing with her hands inside his shirt?

It makes you wonder if there's anything the magical Lyrebird Lake can do for these two strong and proud people who don't know how to let go of the past.

I adored this book. There's a bit of intrigue, a bit of action, the joy of birth, and of course a love story. I loved Tammy, I loved Leon, and I loved the boys—and they all made me smile down to my toes when they interacted with each other.

While this book stands alone, I hope you enjoy your return to the setting of Lyrebird Lake, which has become a very special place for me, and that Tammy and Leon's story warms you too.

I wish you happy reading

Fiona

A mother to five sons, **Fiona McArthur** is an Australian midwife who loves to write. Medical™ Romance gives Fiona the scope to write about all the wonderful aspects of adventure, romance, medicine and midwifery that she feels so passionate about—as well as an excuse to travel! Now that her boys are older, Fiona and her husband Ian are off to meet new people, see new places, and have wonderful adventures. Fiona's website is at www.fionamcarthur.com

Recent titles by the same author:

MIDWIFE IN THE FAMILY WAY*
THE MIDWIFE AND THE MILLIONAIRE
MIDWIFE IN A MILLION
PREGNANT MIDWIFE: FATHER NEEDED*
THE MIDWIFE'S NEW-FOUND FAMILY*

Lyrebird Lake Maternity

Dedication:

For Rosie and Carol, my fabulous friends,
who put up with those phone calls
when I'm stuck.

CHAPTER ONE

As A reluctant best man, Leonardo Durante Bonmarito caught the unashamed adoration on the groom's face as he circled the room with his new bride, and knew his own earlier arrival in Australia would have made no difference.

Leon's intention of stopping this wedding had faltered at the first sight of Gianni at the airport because nothing would have prevented his brother from marrying this woman.

Such happiness made Leon's chest hurt and he'd never liked wedding feasts. It was even harder when he felt insulated from the joy and gaiety around him by the fact he still hadn't had a chance to talk to Gianni properly since arriving.

'Not a big fan of weddings?' The words were mild enough but the tone held a hint of quiet rebuke. Tammy Moore, chief bridesmaid and for tonight his partner, spoke at his shoulder and Leon returned to the present with a jolt. She went on, 'We're supposed to join them on the floor now.'

'*Sì*. Of course. My apologies.' Automatically he glanced around and down and unexpectedly his vision was filled with the delightful valley between her breasts.

He swept his eyes upwards and her dark brows tilted at the flicker of a smile he couldn't help.

It was a problem but what was a man to do with a bodice just under eye level? It would be strange dancing with a woman willow-slim in body and almost as tall as himself. She felt twice the height of his late wife.

He wondered if others might think they

looked good together. Little did observers know their rapport had been anything but cordial, because he feared he hadn't endeared himself to her.

Leon repressed a sigh. He'd barely talked, in fact, it seemed he'd forgotten how to be at ease with a young woman, but in his defence, his mind had been torn between the recent danger to Paulo and when he could discuss it with his brother.

Tammy tapped her foot with the music, surely not with impatience, as she waited for them to join the bride and groom on the floor and he'd best concentrate. He hoped it would not be too much of a disaster because his heart wasn't in it. 'You are very good to remind me,' he said by way of apology, but she didn't comment, just held out one slender hand for him to take so the guests could join in after the official party was on the floor.

The music wheezed around them with great gusto if not great skill, like a jolly asthmatic between inhaler puffs, and Leon took her fingers in his and held them. Her hand lay small and slim, and somehow vulnerable, in his clasp, and suddenly he wasn't thinking of much except the way she unexpectedly fitted perfectly into his arms, her small breasts soft against his chest, and her hair smooth against his face.

In fact, her hip swung against his in seamless timing as if they'd danced together to a breathless piano accordion since birth.

Such precision and magical cadence took him from this place—and his swirling, painful thoughts—to a strange mist of curative tranquillity he'd craved since not just yesterday but from the haze of time in his youth.

Where was the awkwardness that'd always seemed to dog him and his late wife whenever they'd danced? The concept deepened the guilt in his heart and also the frown across his brows.

'You sway like a reed in my arms.' He tilted his head in reluctant approval. 'You must dance often.'

He thought he heard, 'Nearly as often as you frown, you great thundercloud.' The un-expected words were quiet, spoken to his feet, and he must have heard wrong because she fol-lowed that with, 'Yes, we love dancing here.'

He decided he was mistaken, but the humility in her expression had a certain facade of mock innocence, and made his suspicions deepen with amused insight. Then he caught his son's eye as they swept past, and Leon raised his eye-brows at the flower girl standing beside him.

Paulo glanced at the young girl and then back at his father, nodded and took her hand to lead her into the dance. Tammy followed his gaze and smiled stiffly, something, he realised guiltily, she'd been doing for a couple of hours now.

She slanted a glance at him. 'Does your son dance as well as his father?'

They both turned their heads to watch the children waltz and Leon felt the warmth of pride. Paulo did well and it had not been an easy few days for him. 'I hope so. He has been taught. A man must be able to lead.'

'Emma's daughter can hold her own,' she murmured, and he bent his head closer to catch her words. Did the woman talk to him or to herself? An elusive scent, perfectly heated by the satin skin of her ridiculously long neck, curled around his senses with an unexpectedly potent assault. Without thought he closed his eyes and inhaled more deeply. This scent was a siren's weapon, yet she portrayed none of the siren's tricks.

He realised with delay that she'd continued

the conversation. 'We have a bring-a-plate country dance once a month in the old hall. The children enjoy it as much as the adults.'

Leon eased back, he hoped unobtrusively, to clear the opulent fog from his mind but his voice came out deeper than he expected—deeper, lower, almost a caress. 'So dance nights are common in Australia?' What was happening? His brain seemed to have slowed to half speed as if he'd been drugged. Perhaps she did have tricks he was unaware of.

He lifted his head higher and sought out his son. The most important reason he needed his wits about him. Whatever spell she'd cast over him, he did not want it.

No doubt she'd sensed the change in him. He could only hope he'd left her as confused as she'd left him. 'To hold a dance is not un-usual in a country town.' Her dark brows drew together in a glower such as she'd accused him of.

'Of course.' Thankfully, this time, his voice emerged normally, though he wondered if she could hear the ironic twist under the words. 'My brother is full of the virtues of your Lyrebird Lake.' And its incredibly fertile qualities, but he wouldn't go there.

She lifted her chin high and stared into his eyes as if suspicious of his tone and the implication he might disparage her hometown. Her irises were a startling blue and reminded him of the glorious sea on the Amalfi Coast, disturbingly attractive, yet with little waves of tempest not quite concealed and a danger that could not be underestimated. He knew all about that.

She went on in that confident voice of hers that managed to raise the dominant side of him like hairs on his neck. 'Lyrebird Lake has everything I need,' she stated, almost a dare to contradict.

He bit back the bitter laugh he felt churn in his chest. A fortunate woman. 'To have everything you want is a rarity. You are to be congratulated. Even if it seems a little unrealistic for such a young woman with no husband.'

Tammy smiled between gritted teeth. This man had created havoc in her usual calm state since the first moment she'd seen him. Too tall, too darkly handsome with sensually heavy features and so arrogant, so sure of his international power. Fancifully she'd decided he'd surveyed them all as if they were bush flies under an empty Vegemite jar.

One more dance and she was done. She felt like tapping her foot impatiently as she waited for the music to start again now the guests and not just the wedding party filled the floor.

It had been as if he'd barely got time for this

frivolity of weddings, such an imposition to him, but she'd stayed civil because of Emma, and Gianni, obviously the much nicer brother of the two. But soon this last dance would be over, then everyone else would not notice her slip away. The official responsibilities she'd held would be complete apart from helping the bride to change.

No more being nice to Leonardo Bonmarito.

Though Tammy did feel sorry for Paulo Bonmarito, a handsome but quiet and no doubt downtrodden child, and she'd asked her own son to look after him. Nobody could call her Jack downtrodden.

As if conjured by the thought, eight-year-old Jack Moore, another young man resplendent in his miniature wedding tuxedo, walked up to Paulo. They looked almost like brothers, both dark-haired, olive-skinned boys with the occasional awkwardness of prepubescence. Then Jack tapped the young Italian boy on the shoulder as he and Grace waited to begin again. 'My dance now, I think.'

That wasn't what she'd envisaged when she'd said watch out for Paulo. Leon's back was to the children and Tammy frowned as she strained to hear as they stood waiting.

'You said you weren't dancing,' she heard Grace say, and the girl looked unimpressed with swapping for a boy she always danced with.

Jack shrugged as he waited for Paulo to relinquish his partner. 'Changed my mind.'

Without looking at Jack, Paulo bowed over Grace's hand, kissed her fingers in the continental way with practised ease and shrugged. *'Non importo. Grazie,'* he said, and turned with head high and walked away.

The music started and the dance floor shifted

like a sleepy animal awakening. Leon's son leaned with seeming nonchalance against a flower-decked pole and watched Grace being swung around easily by Jack. Like his father, his face remained expressionless and Tammy wondered if Paulo was used to disappointment.

When the dance was over, Tammy eased her hand out of Leon's firm grip as unobtrusively as she could and stepped back. She only just prevented herself from wiping her hand down the side of her bridesmaid dress to try and diffuse the stupid buzz of connection she could still feel.

The contact hadn't been what she expected and the dancing had increased her need to distance herself from this haughty stranger even more. It had been ridiculous the way they'd danced together as if they'd spent years, not seconds, training to synchronise. Not a common occurrence with her local partners but maybe she was imagining it just because he was taller and stronger, and decidedly more masterful, than most men she danced with.

Or maybe the strength of her disquiet about him had made her more aware. Either way she wasn't interested and needed to get away from him to her friends.

'Thank you.' She didn't meet his eyes and instead glanced around at the crowded dance floor. 'Everyone seems to be up now. If you'll excuse me?'

Leon raised one sardonic eyebrow at her apparent haste. 'You have somewhere you need to run off to?'

She opened her mouth to fabricate an excuse when the glowing bride, her best friend, Emma, dragged her smiling new husband across to his brother. 'Tammy! You and Leon dance wonderfully together.' She beamed at her husband, and the look that passed between them made

Tammy glance away with a twist of ridiculous wistfulness.

'Almost as good as us,' Emma went on. 'Isn't my wedding beautiful?'

'Truly magnificent,' Leon said, and glanced at Gianni. 'Your organisational skills exceed even what I expected.'

'Nothing is too perfect for my wife.' Gianni, tall and solid like his brother, stroked Emma's cheek, and then looked across at Tammy. He smiled. 'And your partner for tonight?' He kissed his fingers. *'Bellissimo.* You, too, are blessed, brother. Tammy is another of the midwives here. Has she told you?'

'We've had little time for discussion.' Leon leaned forward and unexpectedly took Tammy's hand in his large one again. He held it firmly and the wicked glint in his eyes when he looked at her said he knew she wouldn't quibble in front of her friend. 'I was just going to find us a drink and sit down for a chat.'

Dear Emma looked so delighted Tammy didn't have the heart to snatch her fingers free, so she smiled, ignored the restart of the buzz in her fingers and wondered bitterly if her teeth would ache tonight from all the clenching she'd done today.

The music started and Gianni held out his hand to his wife. Emma nodded. 'I'll see you back at the bridal table, Tammy, after this dance. I want to tell you something.' Then Emma smiled blithely at them, sighed into her husband's arms and danced away.

Tammy looked around for escape but there was none. Trapped by her friend. Great. Leon held firmly on to her hand and steered her off the floor towards the official table. Unobtrusively Tammy tugged at her fingers and finally he let her hand free. She leaned towards him with a grim smile and, barely moving her lips, let him have it. 'Don't ever do that again or you will get more than you bargained for.'

'Tut. Temper.' He glanced down at her, amused rather than chastened by her warning, which made her more cross.

She grimaced a smile again and muttered, 'You have no idea,' as he pulled her chair out. She slipped into the chair and shifted it slightly so that it faced towards the dance floor and her shoulder tilted away from him.

When he returned with two tiny champagne flutes Leon was fairly sure she didn't realise the angle she gave him lent a delightful view of her long neck and the cleft below the hollow of her throat…and there was that incredible drift of scent again.

He controlled his urge to move closer. This woman had invaded his senses on many un-expected levels and here he was toying with games he hadn't played since his amorous youth.

'Drink your wine,' he said.

She turned to him and her eyes narrowed blue fire at him. 'Were you born this arrogant or did you grow into it?'

So, her temper remained unimproved. She amused him. He shrugged and baited her. 'Bonmaritos have been in Portofino for six generations. My family are very wealthy.'

She lifted one elegant shoulder in imitation. 'Big deal. So were mine and my childhood was less than ideal.'

'And you are not arrogant?' To his surprise she looked at him and then smiled at his comment. And then to his utter astonishment she threw back her head and laughed. A throaty chortle that had his own mouth curve in appreciation.

Her whole face had softened. 'Actually, I've been told I am.'

When she laughed she changed from being a very attractive but moody woman into a delightful seductress he could not take his eyes off, and when she shuffled her chair back and studied him for a change, he felt the shift in their rapport like a fresh breeze. A dangerous, whimsical, warning breeze that he should flee from.

He shifted closer. 'So tell me, Tammy, is this your full name?'

'Tamara Delilah Moore, but nobody calls me that.'

'Delilah I believe. Tamara?' He rolled the name off his tongue as if sampling it, found the taste delightful and he nodded. That suited her better. 'There was a famous noblewoman called Tamara in Roman mythology. She, too, was tall and apparently rather arrogant. How ironic.'

'Really?' She raised those stern eyebrows of hers and Leon realised he liked the way she responded fearlessly to his bait. 'What if I say you're making that up?'

The music lilted around them playfully and helped the mood stay light. 'I would have to defend myself.'

She glanced down at her hands and spread them to look at her fingertips as if absorbed in her French manicure. He almost missed her comment. 'You nearly had to defend yourself in a more physical way earlier.'

So. More fire. He straightened and met her eyes with a challenge. 'I had the utmost faith in your control. You'd exhibited control all day. It's a wonder your teeth aren't aching.'

She blinked, glanced at him with an arrested expression and then laughed again. He felt the smile on his face. A deeper more genuine smile than he'd had for a long time. It felt surprisingly good to make her laugh.

Not something he'd been known for much in the past but her amusement warmed him in a place that had been cold for too long. 'Of course I also have a slight weight advantage.'

'And I have a black belt in karate.' She picked up one of the biscotti favours from a plate on the table and unconsciously broke a piece off, weighing it in her hand before putting it to her mouth. That curved and perfect mouth he'd been trying not to look at for the past ten minutes.

Karate. He searched for an image of sweating women in tracksuits he could call to mind, or the name of the white pyjamalike uniform people wore for martial arts, anything to take his mind off the sight of her lips parting as she absently turned him on.

'How long are you staying before you head back to Italy?' she said carelessly as she raised the biscuit shard. His gaze followed her fingers, drawn by invisible fields of magnetism and, unconsciously, he held his breath. Gi. The uniform was called gi.

Her lips opened and she slid the fragment in and licked the tips of her fingers, oblivious to his fascinated attention as she glanced at the dancers. His breath eased out and his body stirred and stretched in a way it hadn't in a long time.

Then she glanced back at him and he had to gather his scattered wits. When was he leaving? Perhaps sooner than he intended if this was how tempted he'd already become. 'Gianni and Emma are away for the first few days of their honeymoon, and then Paulo and I will join them at the airport before we all return to Italy.' He was rambling.

He focused on the plans he'd finalised before he left for Italy. 'We were held up.' He paused. His grip tightened unconsciously on the glass in his hand and he looked away from her—that brought him back to earth. There was no time for this when the real world required constant and alert attention.

He shook his head and went on. 'We were held up on the way over and arrived later than expected. It will give Paulo a few days to get over the "excitement" before we have to return.' She nodded.

Jack appeared at her side and tugged on her dress. 'Excuse me, Mum. Can we go and play spotlight?'

Tammy looked away from this suddenly much more attractive man to her son and the world started again. What was she thinking? She blinked again to clear her head and swallowed the last of the biscuit. 'Who with?' she asked Jack, and looked beyond him to the milling group of young boys and girls.

'Dawn and Grace, and Peta and Nicky. And some of the older kids as well.' He glanced at Leon. 'And Paulo if he wants to?'

Leon frowned and looked across to where his son was talking to Grace and another girl. 'What is this "spotlight"?'

Tammy shrugged. 'Hide-and-seek in the dark and the seeker has a handheld torch or spotlight. The children play it all the time here when parties like this stretch into evening.'

Leon's frown didn't lighten. 'Even young girls? Without parents supervising?'

'They won't go far.' She looked at Paulo, who pretended he didn't expect his father to say no. 'Let him go. He'll be fine.'

Leon hesitated, and she wondered if he'd been this protective since the boy's mother had died. Overprotecting children made her impatient but she held her tongue, if not her expression, and then finally he nodded.

'Perhaps for a short while.' He tilted his head at his son and Paulo approached them. He spoke in Italian and Tammy looked away but she couldn't help overhearing.

She had no trouble interpreting Leon's discussion with his son. She'd been able to speak Italian since her teenage years in a dingy Italian coffee shop in Sydney, dark with dangerous men and a tall Italian youth she hadn't seen since but wasn't allowed to forget. Those memories reminded her why she wasn't attracted to Leonardo Bonmarito.

'Do you wish to play this game?' Leon said to his son.

'*Sì,*' said Paulo, and he looked away to the other children.

'Be aware of your safety,' Leon continued in his native language, and Tammy frowned at the tablecloth in front of her. It seemed a strange thing to say at his brother's wedding in a country town.

'*Sì, Padre*, of course,' Paulo said again, and when his father nodded he ran off to join the children. Tammy hoped she wiped the expression from her face before she glanced back at Leon. Listening to Leon talk to his son brought back many memories and it had surprised her how easily she slipped back into recognising the words.

'Your son has beautiful manners. Is he allowed to play with other children much?'

It was her turn to be frowned on. 'Of course.' No doubt she'd offended him. Oops, she thought without remorse.

Leon went on in a low, steely voice that made her eyebrows rise. 'He attends school. And your Jack? He appears very confident.' His eyes travelled over her. 'Like his mother.'

She shrugged. Tough if he had a problem with that. 'There's only been Jack and me together, although my father and my stepmother have always been very much a part of his life since he was born. They live next door.'

She saw his gaze drift to his brother and the planes of his angular face softened as he nodded. 'Family is important. Especially when one's family is smaller than God intended.'

There seemed a story there. She wasn't quite sure what he was getting at. Did he have plans to enlarge his family? Was he here to convince his brother to take his wife back to Italy for good? Perhaps it would be better to know one's enemy, as good as an excuse as any for plain old nosiness, but she had to admit to herself he intrigued her. 'So, both your parents are gone?'

'*Sì.*' Reluctance in the answer. 'They died when we were young.'

She should stop the questions, but maybe now a silence would be even more awkward, or that's what she told herself as she asked the next. 'To lose a parent is hard, to lose both would be devastating. Especially as I believe you are the eldest of the two of you?'

He shrugged and his voice had cooled. 'By four years. It was my responsibility to be the head of the family.'

At how old? she wondered. 'No other relatives to look after you?'

He answered almost absently as his attention was distracted by the calls and laughter of the children. 'An elderly widowed aunt who has since passed away.' He frowned again as Paulo ducked with a grin behind a dark bush.

He really did have issues with Paulo playing with the other children, Tammy decided. 'And Emma says you lost your wife last year?'

His gaze snapped back to her and this time

he raised haughty brows at her. *'Molto curioso,'* he said.

Yes, she couldn't deny she was curious. She looked at him blandly as if she had no idea what he said, until he inclined his head and continued on a different topic. 'It is good to see Paulo with a smile on his face. They have been too rare in the past year.'

The pang of sympathy for both of them reminded her of the past as well. 'And now your own son has lost his mother. It's hard to lose your mother.'

Now that brought back memories she'd rather forget but felt obliged to share as she'd been so nosy. 'Even difficult mothers. I was fifteen when I lost mine. Went to live with my mother's mother.' She laughed with little amusement. 'Who said my living there made her feel too old. Such a silly woman.'

'Perhaps it is my turn to be curious?' It

seemed Leon waited for her to enlarge on the topic. Not a hope in Hades.

She said the first thing she could think of to avoid a discussion of her ridiculous past. 'Would you like to dance again?' She discovered as she waited for his answer the idea held definite appeal.

His mouth tilted and she knew he was aware of her sudden change of subject. 'I would like that very much.'

The palpitations came out of nowhere. Just started to thump in her chest as he stood— and from where she sat he filled her vision; he truly was magnificent—then drew her up, with that strong hand of his closing on hers. She felt weightless, like a feather, and a little airy like a feather too, which wasn't like her as she drifted across to the floor where the piano accordion was valiantly attempting to play a waltz.

It was okay to enjoy a dance. With a skilled

partner. Nothing wrong with that. His arms came around her and she closed her eyes, giving in to the moment for once, not fighting the magic that had surprised her earlier in the evening. This was what dancing was for. She just hadn't realised she'd been searching for the right partner.

CHAPTER TWO

TAMMY missed the moment when the music stopped until Leon's arm drifted down her back to her hip and he angled her towards the bridal table. The tiny, secret smile on her face fell away with her trance. How embarrassing.

His fingers were warm on her skin through the thin material of her bridesmaid dress as he led her back to her chair.

Both of them were silent. And that serves me right for letting my guard down, Tammy thought, as she tried to think of something to say that would dispel the myth she'd been lost in his arms.

In the end she was saved by the bride. 'You two seem to be getting along *very* well.' A

glowing Emma grinned at them as she and
Gianni approached the table. When her husband held her chair for her Emma sank thankfully down and fanned her face. She looked
from one to the other but neither spoke.

Leon murmured his thanks as he lifted his
hand in a 'spare me a moment' gesture to his
brother. Then he slanted a glance at Tammy,
his face serious as he caught her eye, before he
and his brother walked off just a few paces.

Tammy saw Leon's glance flick to the boys
as they disappeared around the corner of the
building but her attention was brought back to
the table by Emma's excitement. 'The dancing is such fun.' Emma waved her hand some
more as she tried to stir the warm air. 'Did you
have a good chat with Leon before the dance?
I wondered if you'd find much to talk about.'

'We talked about the boys,' Tammy said, and
then she heard Leon ask Gianni, in Italian, if

he thought the spotlight game was safe enough. He was back to that.

Tammy strained her ears for Gianni's answer, his affirmative clear, but then something Leon said very quietly made Gianni stop suddenly and stare and the two men moved further out of earshot, both bristling, and she had the sudden ridiculous thought that they were like a pair of wolves hunting in the night.

The darkness of a black shadow ran icy fingers over her neck and she shook the feeling off mostly because she didn't do premonitions, and secondly because it wasn't a happy wedding-day vibration at all and a far cry from the heady bubble of the dance floor.

She turned to Emma and worked to dispel the unease that lingered despite her efforts to banish it. 'So what were you so anxious to tell me that I had to sit beside your brother-in-law and wait with bated breath?'

'Poor you. Was he such a hardship?' Emma teased.

Tammy glanced towards the spot where the men had disappeared. 'It's been a long day,' she said cryptically, 'but perhaps he might not be as bad as I thought.'

Emma's brows crinkled. 'Good.' Though now there was a trace of doubt in her voice. 'Because I want everyone to get on well.' Emma looked for the men too, and back at Tammy. Then all the excitement caught up with her again and Tammy vowed to be more careful not to blemish her friend's day.

'My news?' She smiled happily. 'Well, first Leon's talking to your father about some project in Rome so he and Paulo are not flying back immediately.'

Tammy knew that, and didn't see much there to be excited about. She didn't like the uncomfortable feeling the man left her with.

Emma bubbled on. 'So Leon and Paulo are staying here until after we come back from our mini honeymoon and then we're going to Italy for a month's holiday. Gianni asked if in a couple of weeks you and Jack might like to come over and be with me while he has to sort out work commitments with his brother.'

Tammy raised her eyebrows and her friend went on. 'So Grace and I won't get bored?' Emma looked at her expectantly. 'What do you think?'

What did she think? That this was the last thing she'd expected. Did she want to go to Italy? While she could admit Emma's new husband had turned out to be a delightful and doting husband, initially she hadn't been overly impressed with his brother.

And now it was more the effect he had on her that had her squirming to find a matching excitement her friend would like. 'I guess

I'd have to think about it. See if Montana has enough staff to cover at the birth centre, work out which of my birthing women are due.'

She shook her head. 'Take Jack overseas? I don't know.' To Italy of all places.

Emma nodded her understanding. 'Think about it. Oh, and I gave Leon your mobile number. Hope you don't mind. In case we're out of range and he needs something.' Emma seemed to think it was no great moment. She was still focused on the Italian trip. 'It's just an idea but I love the sound of both of us in Italy.'

Tammy could see she did. And normally she'd like the idea too. Overseas travel was something she'd done a lot of in her early teens with her parents and she'd been to Italy once. Maybe that had been the start of her attraction to Italians. She tried not to think of him having her number and then decided he didn't look like a stalker. He only had a few days to stalk anyway.

The men came back, both faces too angled and sombre for a wedding feast, though Gianni smiled at his wife when he reached her side. He held out his hand. 'Do you still wish to circulate through the guests, *cara*? I believe a few of the older guests are starting to leave.'

Emma allowed herself to be drawn up and against her husband's chest for a brief hug, as if the two of them had spent a day apart and not a few minutes, and Tammy couldn't help but wonder if she'd ever have such a love as that. She damped down the almost irresistible urge to sneak a glance at Leon's face to see what he was thinking. When she did he was looking at her and for some bizarre reason her face flamed.

Thankfully, her friend seemed oblivious to Tammy's own embarrassment as she stepped, pink-cheeked, back out of her husband's arms. 'I haven't spent much time with Louisa. Shall we see her before she goes?'

'Indeed.' Gianni smiled warmly. 'I will inquire if she thinks my brother can be as excellent a guest as when I stayed with her.'

They walked away and Leon sat down. She saw him again seek the boys out in the shadows. 'Everything okay?' Tammy searched his face but the mask he'd arrived with earlier in the day was firmly back in place. She could read nothing and it irritated her for no good reason.

He inclined his head. 'Of course.'

'So you and Paulo have settled into the old doctor's residence with Louisa for a few days?'

'She has made us very welcome.' This time he did smile and the sudden warmth in his eyes did strange, unsettling things to her stomach.

Things she hadn't had a problem with for nearly ten years. Maybe she was hungry. Though that seemed unlikely as the wedding feast had more choices than a country fete.

The thought came out of nowhere. What would he be like to kiss? Her belly twisted. Great, she'd bet. He had amazing lips, like sculptured marble on a work of art. Good grief. She checked out her nails again, to hide her eyes.

He went on. 'Paulo has never had so many affectionate embraces and we have only been there since last night.'

'Louisa loves a cuddle.' It was amazing she could carry on a conversation and be so focused on his mouth. She risked a glance. 'She's a recent widow.' Yep, they still looked good.

Leon concentrated on Louisa, whom he could see behind the dancers, the little woman who'd made his son so welcome, and thankfully the tension eased. He wasn't sure where it came from but he'd felt the sudden rise between them. 'My brother told me of her loss. And that is why he asked we stay there. It is no hardship.'

He kept his eyes on his brother and his wife across the floor. In fact, even this wedding had become no hardship. It was surprising how re-signed he'd become to his brother's fate. And in a few short hours, partly because no one could doubt the true bond between the newlyweds, and partly because all of the people he'd met here tonight had exuded such warmth and gen-erosity towards him and his son.

Except this woman.

The thought made him smile for some reason, as if the challenge for supremacy between them had taken on a new urgency. He fought the errant concept away. No. Perhaps it had been too long since he had set aside time to share intimacy with a woman. The chance of a brief liaison with this Tamara was tantalising but remote. Too much was happening.

And she would be the last to welcome him. The thought made him smile again. He'd somehow offended her, and he searched his memory for that ridiculous saying he'd heard today—he'd got up her nose. And such a delightful nose it was. He smiled again. She was not showing a warm or generous side to him at all but he perceived she had one, which in fact was lucky, because he became more intrigued every minute he spent with her.

Tammy saw him smile at the thought of Louisa. So he did have a soft spot for elderly widows. The idea dangerously thawed a little more of her reserve and she reached for another unwanted biscuit to distract her concentration from this handsome, brooding man beside her.

She felt his attention and when she glanced at him there was a sudden darkening of his eyes that arrowed that sharp sensation of hunger right back through her midsection. She felt the wave of heat between them like a furnace door opening.

'Not again,' he murmured. And then more strongly, 'If you delicately consume another biscotti I will not be responsible for my actions.' His voice was very quiet, and she realised they were alone at the table—in fact, alone at their side of the dance floor. The children shrieked with laughter in the distance just in view, Emma and Gianni were across talking to Louisa, and suddenly she couldn't look away from him. Her stomach kicked again. She got the message.

She wasn't sure what to do now with the biscuit she didn't want, but blowed if she'd let him know he'd rocked her.

Did she look away and nonchalantly put it down or did she pull the tiger's tail? There was no choice really.

Unhurriedly, with great deliberation, Emma raised the shard of almond to her mouth. With her eyes on his she parted her lips with seductive exaggeration and slid it slowly in, and chewed. It was hard to swallow with a dry mouth but she did. Choking would have ruined the impact. To drive home her point she calmly licked the sugar from her finger. One raised eyebrow left him in no doubt of her message. *Don't dare me.*

Leon stood, took the arm that reached towards him—surely she hadn't asked her fingers to do that—and Tammy found herself whisked back into the shadows with her hand in his. In an instant she was in his arms and his body felt warm and inflexible against hers. It had all happened so fast she doubted anyone had noticed she'd been abducted.

His eyes glittered in the low light. 'You do not follow orders well, I think.' She barely heard him over the thumping in her chest as he stared down at her, and there was something primal about the tree branch casting shadows across his face. 'This night has been filled with intriguing moments. I cannot allow it to conclude without this.' He bent his dark head towards her with such intent she froze as he brushed her neck with his lips. She shivered and all the hair on her arms whooshed into an upright position on little mountains of goose flesh.

'Your scent has been driving me wild all night.' His words hummed against her ear and thrummed down her throat as his lips travelled the sensitive skin around her jaw. She'd never felt exposed and vulnerable and yet starving for more.

His mouth took flight across her cheek like a hot moth that dusted both eyes before homing in on her mouth. Every nerve in her skin seemed to lean his way for attention, drawn to the light like a kamikaze insect, and she shuddered at the delicious sensations his whispered caress invoked.

Somehow her arms had wound themselves round his neck and she could feel the sinew and muscle in his shoulders, rock hard beneath her fingers. He had the power to snap her in two and they both knew it.

Then his mouth found hers, her stomach jolted and she swayed against him suddenly weak at the knees like an old-fashioned heroine. She'd never believed this would happen to her. A swoon from a man kissing her. It was ridiculous, and crazy, and…

* * *

'It was a funny wedding,' Jack said as he drove home with his mother.

'Funny in what way?' Tammy said extremely absently as she turned along the sweeping driveway out of the lakeside complex. When Leon had kissed her Tammy realised what she'd been missing for too many years. She'd kissed a few men, more to reassure herself she could get a man to the point, but never been enamoured enough to want to repeat the experience.

With Leonardo Bonmarito she'd wanted to do more than repeat it. She wanted next verse. Next chapter. The whole darn book and she knew where that could leave her. She prayed he hadn't realised because she'd managed to step back before she'd dragged the buttons from his shirt. But only just. So she'd stepped away further, called her son and left fairly quickly after that.

'Just different.' The childish voice beside her

reminded her why she'd stepped away. 'And that kid's different too.'

'Paulo? I imagine they'd be saying the same thing about you if you turned up at a wedding in Italy.'

She glanced at Jack. Her miniature man in the house, whom she adored but had no blinkers about. 'Which reminds me, you were impolite to push into that dance with Grace and Paulo.'

He looked away from her and squirmed a little. 'She didn't want to dance with him.'

'That's not what I saw.'

Jack sniffed and avoided his mother's glance. 'She danced with him later anyway,' he muttered.

Tammy dimmed her lights for a passing car. 'I wouldn't like to think you were rude or acting the bully to a visitor, Jack.'

'I don't like him.' More muttering.

Tammy frowned. Jealous brat. 'Even more reason to be nice to him.'

Jack sniffed again. 'Like you were nice to his father?'

Now where had that come from? Thank goodness it was dark and he couldn't see the pink flooding her neck. Little ankle biter. She certainly wasn't going there. Of course the children hadn't seen. 'Yes.' She took the easy way out. 'Did you all have fun playing spotlight?'

She caught the movement of his shoulder beside her as he shrugged. 'He was scared half the time.'

The dark cloud of uneasiness slid new tendrils through her mind. Tammy glanced at her son and then back at the road. 'Why do you think he was scared?'

Jack swivelled and she could tell without turning her head that he was looking at her. 'What would you do if a man tried to kidnap me?'

Tammy blinked at the unexpected question and her hands tightened until they were almost white on the wheel. Someone take her son? Harm Jack? Threaten to kill him? 'Tear him limb from limb.' She shook the power of the unexpected passion off. Good grief, there'd been some emotional roller-coasters tonight. 'What made you ask that?'

Such a little voice from the darkness. 'He said it sometimes happens in Italy for ransom money.'

'Who? Paulo?' She'd read of it but didn't want to think about such a crime actually happening. Europe was a long way from Lyrebird Lake. 'Well, let's hope someone doesn't want to ransom you.'

Then he said it. Explained it. Let loose the cloud that turned from dark to black. 'Just before they left to come to Australia somebody tried to take Paulo. That's why they didn't get here till yesterday.'

That couldn't be true. 'What do you mean? Who did?' She slowed the car, then slowed it some more, which didn't really matter because there wasn't that much traffic around Lyrebird Lake. It would be better if she didn't run into anyone.

'They don't know. His father caught them before they could get away but they put a bag over Paulo's head and knocked him out.'

Tammy's heart thumped under her ribs and she shivered at the thought of someone attempting to steal a child. Any child. Her child.

Then she remembered how she'd been less than diplomatic about Leon's reluctance with the children's game and she winced. Every instinct urged her to turn the car around and apologise to Leon for her ill judgement. Poor

Paulo, poor Leon. And the kidnappers had struck a child. 'Paulo told you this?'

Jack was losing interest. 'No, Grace did. Paulo told her.'

Good grief. No wonder Leon hadn't wanted him to play spotlight. It was amazing he'd let his son out of his sight at all. She glanced at Jack. 'If that's true, even you should understand why he was scared in spotlight.'

'I guess.' He looked at his mother. 'You'd find me, wouldn't you, Mum?'

She stretched her arm across and ruffled his hair with her fingers. The strands were fine and fragile beneath the skin of her fingertips and the sheer fragment of the concept of losing him tightened a ball of fear in her chest. 'I wouldn't rest until I did.'

Jack snuggled down in his seat. 'I thought so,' he said, and yawned loudly.

* * *

Tammy was glad to get to work the next morning. The night had been a sheet-crunching wrestle for peace that she'd only snatched moments of and this morning a rush to get a tired and cross Jack through the fence to Misty's house.

Leon Bonmarito had a lot to answer for. She'd walked straight into a birth and thankfully hadn't given the man a thought for the past three hours.

Tammy wrapped the squirming newborn infant in a fluffy white towel and tucked him under her arm like a football. Little dark eyes blinked up at her out of the swathe and one starfish hand escaped to wave at her. She tucked the tiny fingers in again and ran the water over his head as she brushed the matted curls clean. She grinned at his mother. 'I haven't seen such thick hair for a long time.'

Jennifer Ross watched with adoration as the

little face squinted and frowned at the sensation in his scalp. 'He's gorgeous.' She sighed and rubbed her stomach and her son turned his head in her direction.

'Thanks for rinsing his hair for me, Tammy. I'm just not up to it.' Even in the dimly lit corner of the room where the sink nestled Tammy could see him try to focus on the familiar sound of his mother's voice.

'We'll just use water today. We'll bath Felix properly tomorrow so we don't overload his poor nose with baby bath perfume.' Tammy combed a little curl onto his forehead and smiled. 'He needs to feel secure, with your skin and his smelling the same as he remembers from inside you. It all helps with establishing breastfeeding. Like the way you waited for him to find the breast and didn't push him on for that first feed.'

'I can't believe he moved there himself.' Jen's face was soft with wonder.

'He'll do it again too. That's why it's better not to wash your own hair with shampoo the first twenty-four hours. A strong scent like shampoo has can confuse and even upset his nose during that time.'

'I'll let Ken's mum know when I ring her. She likes a heavy perfume but she's a sweetie. She'll give it a miss if I ask.' Jen reached out and touched his little hand that had escaped again. 'I remember when you told my sister only Mum and Dad should snuggle babies for the first twenty-four hours. She swears her second baby is much more settled.'

'Best practice. But sometimes it's hard to manage when everyone wants a hold.'

Jen rubbed her stomach again. 'Better to do it right. If the after pains get much worse I might not have a third one,' Jen said with a rueful smile.

'Have a lie-down. You've had a big day and there's a warm wheat pack on your bed. I'll bring Felix in when I've dressed him and check your tummy.' She cast her eye over the mum and decided she looked okay. 'Let me know if you start to bleed more heavily.'

'Thanks, I'll do that.' Jen smiled and turned gingerly with her hand holding her stomach. 'I'm looking forward to that wheat pack. Ken's so disappointed he wasn't home for the birth. And I have to ring his mother and sister as well.'

'Since when do babies wait for truck-driving daddies? Ken will just be glad you're both well. Off you go. I'll be in soon.' She narrowed her gaze as the other woman hobbled out. Tammy wished Ken could have made it too. She wanted every mother's birth to be perfect for them but sometimes babies just didn't wait.

When Ben brought Leon in to see the unit Tammy had just towelled Felix's hair dry. She was laughing down at him as she tried to capture the wriggling limbs and they'd moved to the sunny side of the room as she began to dress him. The early-afternoon sunlight dusted her dark hair with shafts of dancing light and her skin glowed.

For Leon, suddenly the day was brighter and even more interesting, although his tour of the facilities had captured his attention until now. Strangely all thoughts of bed numbers, ward structure and layout seemed lower in his priorities than watching the expressions cross this woman's face. And brought back the delightful memory of a kiss that had haunted him long into the night in his lonely bed.

'Hi, there, Tam,' Ben said as he crossed the room. Tammy looked up at her father and smiled. Then she looked at Leon and the smile fell away. He watched it fall and inexplicably the room dimmed.

'Hi, Dad. Leon.' She looked at her father. Or perhaps she was avoiding looking at him, Leon surmised, and began another mind waltz of piqued interest that this woman seemed to kick off in him. 'What are you men up to?'

'I'm showing Leon the facilities. His board's been thinking of adding maternity wards to their children's hospitals and I thought you might like to hint him towards a more woman-friendly concept.'

Leon watched the ignition of sharper concentration and the flare of captured interest. She couldn't hide the blue intensity in her eyes and silently he thanked Ben for knowing his daughter so well. So, Leon mulled to himself, he'd suddenly become a much more interesting person?

'Really?' She tossed it over her shoulder, as if only a little involved, but she couldn't fool him—he was learning to read her like a conspiracy plot in a movie, one fragmented clue at a time.

She dressed the baby with an absentminded deftness that reassured the infant so much he lay compliant under her hands. Mentally Leon nodded with approval. To handle infants a rapport was essential and he was pleased she had the knack, though it was ridiculous that such a thing should matter to him.

When the newborn was fully clothed she nestled him across her breasts and Leon had a sudden unbidden picture of her with her own child, a Madonnalike expression on her face, and a soft smile that quickened his heart.

More foolishness and he shook his head at the distraction the fleeting vision had caused.

Tammy tilted her determined chin his way and Madonna faded away with a pop. 'I'll just take this little bundle into his mother and come back.'

He watched her leave the room, the boyish yet confident walk of an athletic woman, not a hint of the shrinking violet or diffident underling, and he was still watching the door when she returned. That confidence he'd first seen was there in spades. She owned the room. It seemed he activated her assertiveness mechanism. He couldn't help the smile when she returned.

She saw it and blushed. Just a little but enough to give him the satisfaction of discomfiting her and he felt a tinge of his awareness that he'd felt the need to do so.

She looked away to her father and then

back at him. 'What sort of unit were you looking at?'

Enough games. 'Small. One floor of the
building. Midwife run and similar to what your
father has explained happens here, though with
an obstetrician and paediatrician on call because we have that luxury in the city.'

He went on when her interest continued.
'It would be situated in a wing of the private
children's hospital we run now. The medical
personnel cover is available already, as are con-
sulting rooms and theatres.'

She nodded as if satisfied with his motives
and he felt ridiculously pleased. 'We promote
natural birth here and caseload midwifery. Do
the women in your demographic want that sort
of service? What's your caesarean rate, because
ours is the lowest in Australia.' She was defiant
this morning. Raising barriers that hardened
the delicate planes of her face and kept her

eyes from his. He began to wonder why she,
too, felt the need. *Molto curioso.*

'I'm not sure of the caesarean rate—obstet-
rics is not my area—but in my country most
of our maternity units are more in the medical model and busy. Often so understaffed and
underfinanced that the families provide most
of the care for the women after birth.'

Tammy nodded and spoke to her father. 'I'd
heard that. One of my friends had a baby in
Rome. She said the nurses were lovely but very
busy.'

He wanted her to look back at him. 'That is
true of a lot of hospitals. This model would be
more midwifery led for low-risk women.' He
paused, deliberately, before he went on, and
she did bring her gaze back his way. Satisfied,
he continued. 'Of course, my new sister-in-law,
Emma, is also interested and I believe there is
a small chance you and your son could come

to Italy in a few weeks?' He lifted the end of the sentence in a question. 'Perhaps the two of you could discuss what is needed and what would work in my country that is similar to what you have here.'

Tammy intercepted the sudden interest from her father and she shook her head at Ben. 'I haven't even thought much about the chance of travelling in Italy.' Liar. The idea had circled in her head for most of the night. 'I won't say your idea of setting up midwife-led units isn't exciting.' *But that's all that's exciting and you're the main drawback.* She repeated the last part of the sentence to herself. 'But thanks for thinking of me.'

He shrugged those amazing shoulders of his, the memory of which she'd felt under her hands more than once through the night despite her attempts to banish the weakness, and she frowned at him more heavily.

'It is for my own benefit after all,' he said.

She remembered Jack's disclosure, and the idea she'd had to apologise if she saw him, but it wasn't that easy. All the time they talked, at the back of her mind, she wanted to ask about Paulo, about the truth in Jack's revelation, and to admit she hadn't understood his reserve and his protectiveness. But it didn't seem right with her father there just in case Leon didn't wish to discuss it. Or she could just let it go.

She owed him an apology. 'Maybe we could meet for lunch and talk more about your idea,' she offered, though so reluctantly it seemed as if the words were teased out of her like chewing gum stuck on a shoe. He must have thought so because there was amusement in his voice as he declined.

'Lunch, no. I'm away with your father for the rest of the day but perhaps tonight, for dinner?' His amusement was clearer. 'If I pick you up?

My brother and I share a taste in fast cars and we could go for a drive somewhere to eat out.'

She did not want to drive somewhere with this guy. A car. Close confines. Him in control. 'No, thank you.' Besides. It was her invitation and her place to say where they met. 'You could come to my house, it's easier. Bring Paulo if he'd like to come and he can play with Jack.'

She had a sudden vision of her empty pantry and mentally shrugged. 'At six-thirty? I'm afraid Jack and I eat early or I can't get him to bed before nine.'

He shook his head. 'That does not suit.'

Tammy opened her eyes slow and wide at his arrogance and his inability to accept she wanted to set the pace and choose a place that would be safe.

But he went on either oblivious or determined to have his own way. 'I will come after nine.

When Paulo, too, is in bed. I am away all day tomorrow and we will be able to discuss things without small ears around us.'

Tammy caught the raised eyebrows and stifled smile on her father's face and frowned. She'd never been good at taking orders. She bit back the temptation to say nine didn't suit her, but apart from being different to what she usually did, she never slept till midnight anyway.

It would be churlish to stick to her guns. This once she'd let him get away with organising but he wouldn't be making a habit of it.

She conceded, grudgingly. 'I don't normally stay up late but a leisurely after-dinner coffee could be pleasant.'

'I'll see you tonight, then.' He inclined his head and Tammy did the same while Ben looked on with a twinkle in his eye. Tammy glared at her father for good measure which only made his eyes twinkle more as they left.

Tammy could hear the suddenly vociferous new arrival in with his mother and, glad of the diversion, she hastened to the ward to help Jen snuggle Felix up to her breast. She couldn't help the glance out the ward window as the two men crossed the path to the old doctor's residence.

She'd always thought her father a big man but against Leon he seemed suddenly less invincible. It was a strange feeling and she didn't like it. Or maybe she didn't like being so aware of the leashed power of Leonardo Bonmarito.

CHAPTER THREE

Leon arrived at nine.

'So, tell me about your private hospitals. What made you choose paediatrics as a main focus?'

Be cool, be calm, say something. Leon made her roomy den look tiny and cramped. Not something she'd thought possible before. Tammy had run around madly when Jack had gone to bed and hidden all the school fundraising newsletters and flyers in a big basket and tossed all evidence of her weekly ironing into the cupboard behind the door.

She'd even put the dog basket out on the back verandah. Stinky didn't like men. Then she'd put the Jack Russell out in the backyard and spent ten minutes changing her clothes and tidying her hair. Something else she hadn't thought of before at this time of night.

But now she sat relaxed and serene, externally anyway, and watched Leon's passion for his work flare in his eyes. She could understand passion for a vocation; she had it herself, for midwifery and her clients in Lyrebird Lake.

'It's the same in a lot of hospitals in the public system. The lack of staff, age of buildings and equipment and overcrowding means the convalescing patient is often cared for with less attention than necessary. With children that is doubly tragic.'

She couldn't help but admire his mastery of English. Her understanding of Italian was more than adequate but her conversational ability was nowhere near as fluent and his occasional roll of the *r*'s made his underlying accent compellingly attractive. It did something to her insides. She obviously had a dangerous fetish for Italians.

'This has concerned me,' he went on, 'and especially in paediatrics because children are vulnerable, more so when they are sick.'

That brought her back to earth. Children were vulnerable. He had great reason to believe that after Paulo's incident but she'd get around to that. Get around to the fact she'd thought him overprotective. 'I can see what you're getting at. It's hard because of priorities with those more ill. But I agree a lonely and convalescing child needs special care.'

He sat forward in his chair and his shirt tightened impressively across his chest. She didn't want to notice that. *'Sì.'* He was obviously pleased with her. 'There is a shortage of empathetic time for those children on the mend but not yet well enough to go home. I had hoped to prevent their stay from becoming

a more traumatic experience than necessary.'
He glanced up to see if she agreed and she
nodded.

He was determined to ensure his goals were
realised. 'This is especially important if these
children are dealing with other issues, such as
grief from loss of loved ones, or difficult family
circumstances.'

There was an added nuance in his voice that
spoke of history and vast experience. An aver-
sion to children suffering, perhaps more personal than children he'd seen in wards. The
reason teased at her mind. 'Was there something in particular that made you so aware?'

His answer seemed to come from another
direction. 'In our family all sons have entered
the medical profession, though disciplines were
left to our personal preferences. My grandfather was intrigued by surgery, my father
ophthalmology. My passion lies with paediatrics

and Gianni's with emergency medicine. Paolo's area is yet to be discerned.'

That made her smile. 'Paulo's a bit young to be worrying about disciplines, don't you think? I doubt Jack would have a thought in his head about what he'll do when he grows up.'

Leon shook his head. 'In Italy a man learns at an early age that he will be responsible for others.'

'Like dancing,' she suggested. 'A man must be able to lead?'

He returned her smile. '*Sì.*'

She couldn't resist teasing him again. 'So you turned your father's eye hospitals into paediatric wards?'

He raised one stern eyebrow but something made her wonder if he was secretly smiling. 'You do not really think that I would?'

There was a lot going on below the surface here. From both of them. She shook her head.

'No.' He wouldn't do that. She knew little of him but already she could tell he would hold his father's wish to provide service to the blind sacrosanct. 'So the eye hospitals are thriving.'

There it was. A warm and wicked grin that wrapped around her like a cloak dropping over her shoulders. A cloak that enveloped her in all the unusually erotic thoughts that had chased around her head for far too long last night in bed. She was in trouble.

'*Sì*. I built more hospitals. Designed especially for children and staffed with nurses who have much to offer an ailing or grieving child.'

He leaned back in the chair and the fine fabric of his handmade shirt again stretched tight across his chest. He picked up the tiny espresso coffee she'd made for him, black and freshly ground from the machine she couldn't live without, and sniffed it appreciatively.

He took a sip, and those large hands looked incongruous around the tiny cup. *'Perfetto.'*

She'd learned to make good coffee years ago and it was her one indulgence. She dragged her eyes away from his hands because down that road lay danger.

She remembered he and Gianni were orphans and the pieces fell into place. 'How did your parents die, Leon?'

She had connected with his previous statement and why she could sense and understand meanings so easily from a man she barely knew was a puzzle she didn't want to fathom. She wondered if it worried him as much as it worried her.

To her relief he didn't try to avoid her question. 'My parents drowned off the Amalfi Coast from our yacht in a storm.'

Drowned. Poor little boys. 'Storms at sea.' She sighed. 'Mother Nature's temper can be wild and indiscriminate,' she said softly. His eyes gazed off into the distance and she was with him. She could almost feel the spray in her face and hear the scream of the wind and she nodded. 'I've lived by the sea. The weather can be unexpected and fierce. My father still has a house on a fabulous beach, but even he nearly drowned one day when he was washed off the rocks.'

He was watching her, listening to her voice, but she could tell half of him was in another place. 'What happened with you and Gianni?'

He looked through her and his voice dropped. 'Gianni almost died, and I, too, had pneumonia.' She glanced at his face and couldn't help but be touched by his effort to remain expressionless.

'And you were both in hospital afterwards?'

Spoken gently, because she didn't want to break the spell.

He nodded and now she understood where his empathy for those in similar circumstances had grown from because she could see the suppressed emotion, even in the careful blankness. That concept hit her hard, in mutual empathy from her early teens and the scars she still bore. 'How old were you when they died?'

Leon shrugged the pain away. 'Fourteen.' Grieving, convalescing, in a hospital that was rushed and old and unintentionally uncaring. With a ten-year-old brother he'd nearly lost as well.

She could see he knew she'd connected the dots. And wasn't happy. 'It is better in my hospitals now.' He changed the subject. 'To see what you do here, in your maternity section, is good too.'

She allowed the change of subject, aware

instinctively how privileged she'd been to glimpse into the private man and sensitive to his need to close the subject. 'The maternity hospital concept is an exciting idea. I'll certainly talk to Emma about it.'

No doubt he would also be happy because it would mean his brother's new wife would be interested in staying more often in Italy. She didn't fully trust his superior motives without a thought for his ulterior ones.

He was watching her again and she wondered what he'd seen of her thoughts. Not much, she hoped.

'So you, too, have suffered the loss of a parent?' His turn to pry. 'You said you lost your mother young, also?'

Not going there. Fifteen hadn't been a good age to be allowed to run free. 'Yes.' The less said there, the better.

'And that you lived with your grandmother?'

So he remembered. Deep creases marred his forehead. 'Why did you not go with your father when your mother died?'

'It's a long story and maybe another day.' She and her father would have preferred that and maybe her life would have been different. She shrugged her shoulders for something she'd no control over. Fifteen had also been a bad age to be told Ben wasn't her real father.

Rebellion saw Tammy spend many hours loitering at that Italian coffee shop. Months had passed without her father's knowledge of how little supervision her grandmother had exercised.

Rides in fast cars she later found out were stolen. Dark and dangerous men that even her boyfriend was wary of. Secret meetings she'd had to stay silent in.

The day Ben, her father in all that counted if not legally, had arrived to rescue her.

He'd picked her up from the coffee shop when she'd rung him to say she was pregnant and whisked her to Lyrebird Lake. He'd told her then they were petty criminals. Not long later she'd read that her baby's father had been sent to jail for a long time.

No wonder she'd found it all so dreadfully, horribly exciting. That risk-taking and foolish time in her life was something she'd buried when she'd become a responsible mother.

Until Gianni had arrived in Lyrebird Lake and wooed her best friend, she'd covered the Italian episode in her life. Hadn't even tried her language skills out on Gianni so she doubted there was anyone except her father, and maybe his wife, Misty, in Lyrebird Lake who knew her secret.

Emma's betrothal had been such a whirlwind affair she hadn't even mentioned it when her friend had fallen for Gianni.

But she had Jack. The light in her life. And she'd change nothing now. Except maybe the subject again.

She had other motives for asking him here and he'd stayed a while already. 'There's something I want to ask you, though you may not want to discuss it. Something that means I should apologise for my presumption without knowing the facts.'

He frowned and inclined his head.

She hesitated, because she didn't really know him or how he'd react, and then typically, she dived in anyway. 'Was Paulo almost abducted before you came here?'

His brows snapped together. 'Who told you this?'

She straightened in her seat, refusing to be cowed. 'Paulo mentioned it to Emma's daughter, Grace.' She didn't say Grace had told Jack and Jack had told her.

His hand tightened on the cup he held and for a fleeting moment she had the ridiculous thought he might crush it without realising. Surely a man's hand couldn't really do that? In the silence she imagined she could hear the porcelain creak in protest.

'This is true.' He glanced at his white fingers and carefully put the cup down, then ran his other hand through thick black curls. She glimpsed the flicker of white-hot fury in his eyes and it was a warning of what he would be capable of. Strangely she had no problem with that. She'd almost pity the men who tried to harm his son if he caught them.

'I was stupidly distracted by my wish to arrive well before the wedding and took too little care. We are not the first family to be targeted by those who wish to benefit financially from people they see as too wealthy.'

So it was true. The thought made her want

to clutch at her throat but she kept her hands together in her lap as if to hold onto the pictures that wanted to rise up and fill her mind. 'Good grief. What about the police?'

He inclined his head but the movement was noncommittal. 'The police do their best to capture these criminals but by then it is often too late for the one abducted. This will not happen to my son or anyone in my family. I have a private investigator and bodyguards working with me full-time now. Experienced operatives whose records are impeccable and that I trust with my and my family's lives.'

There was almost an aura around him and she recognised the implacable determination that would see him succeed in whatever he set his mind to. 'So you believe Paulo is safe, now that these people work for you?'

He inclined his head. 'Already they have paid tenfold for the money I retain them with. Those responsible have been passed over to the police. Paulo is safe now. No more at risk than any other boy, but it is hard not to look into the dark for danger.'

Who were these Bonmaritos her friend had bound herself to? These superficially cultured men who hid wolves beneath their Italian suits and hired bodyguards. More gangsters she'd fallen in with? Or truly philanthropic doctors merely protecting their own from a culture she didn't understand.

'This all sounds very James Bondish. Not something Lyrebird Lake would ever have to worry about.' She said it firmly, and perhaps a little too quickly, but she really didn't want to think of this scenario in her own home. In the lives of people she knew. In the man opposite her she was strangely drawn to. Dark forces she never wanted to be involved with again. It was too unsettling.

'So my brother says. He does not believe I need the bodyguards here but, for the moment, it is for me. These and other reasons are perhaps why my brother and I should return to our homeland.'

Surely nothing would happen here? In Australia? She didn't like any of this conversation and regretted what she'd discovered. She wondered if Emma was aware of the more menacing undercurrents of the Bonmarito family. 'This seems a long way from discussing children's hospitals and maternity wings.'

Visibly Leon forced his shoulders to relax. 'I'm sorry, Tamara. I apologise if I've upset you. I still struggle with allowing Paulo out of my sight.' But his face remained changed. Harshly angled and fierce. The face of the stranger he really was.

Her chin was up as if she needed to rise and meet the challenge of this warrior of a man.

He didn't frighten her but she gave him the respect he deserved. 'And I apologise for judging your need to know where Paulo was the other night.'

He inclined his head. 'You could not know.' While the dangerous side to this handsome Italian made her uneasy, it was less upsetting when she thought of her own response when Jack had asked what she would do—limb from limb seemed pretty similar to Leon's response. 'The lives of children should be protected.'

'*Sì*. And I should go to check Paulo. It is late.' He stood and she rose also, and couldn't squash the tiny irresponsible hope he would kiss her before he left. She walked him to the door and paused as she opened it. When she turned to him some of the hardness had faded from his face but there was enough of the wolf in him to still keep her head up as she met his eyes.

He had no difficulty seeing into her mind.

His brows lifted. 'Do you want to play dare again, little one?'

So he thought she was little? Danger shuddered deliciously along her veins and made her remember a time in her dim past when she'd put her ear to a train track, the early rumbles of an approaching train, the danger, the paralysing fear that screamed to move. 'Should I in this mood you're in?'

He stepped in. 'That is enough answer for me.'

This kiss was different. Harder, decidedly more dominant with her crushed against his chest, and she pulled him against herself more to keep her feet on the ground and show she wasn't subdued by him. But she was. They leaned into each other, searching out secrets, showing each other hidden facets of their souls rarely exposed like little shafts of moonlight illuminating the areas used to darkness. All the more penetrating because there was no future in it.

When he left her, she leaned her forehead against the closed door with her eyes shut and listened to his car purr away in the darkness.

'Hit by the train,' she murmured into the darkness.

The next day as Tammy worked her early shift in the birthing centre she found herself glancing out the windows whenever she heard male voices, and once she saw her father in the distance with Leon, two dark heads together. One that made her smile and one that burned her with the heat of that last hard kiss.

It was strange how Leon and Ben seemed to find a common ground and mutual respect when there was a good fifteen years difference in age. And she trusted Ben's instincts implicitly so Leon must be 'good people'.

Her stepmother, Misty, the second of the midwives to move to Lyrebird Lake Birthing Centre, arrived to take over the shift. She joined Tammy on the steps to wave goodbye to this morning's new family.

'So Gloria did well.' They walked inside together and Misty grinned down at the birth register open on the desk. 'And they finally have a daughter?'

'In the bath at 10:00 a.m. She came out in three pushes and Gloria's over the moon with how much better this birth was.'

Misty ran her finger along the page and raised her eyebrows at the baby's weight. 'Lovely. And you're dropping there after work?'

Tammy bulldog-clipped the folder she'd completed. 'I said around four. Give them all time to have a sleep. I said I'd pick up their Jimmy after school and give him a chance to meet his new sister.'

'Sounds great.' Misty glanced at her with an unusual thoroughness and Tammy felt as if her stepmother chose her words carefully. 'Your father seems very impressed with Gianni's brother.'

'I was thinking that this morning.' Tammy looked back at Misty with a smile. 'What're your instincts?' There was more to the question than seemed on the surface. By 'instincts' Tammy meant those intangible nuances Misty was known for. Or even more to the point, had Misty had any of those eerie premonitions she occasionally experienced with startling accuracy?

Tammy didn't try to understand Misty's special gift, just accepted it for the reality it was and the fact that Misty had shown on occasion how useful her premonitions could be.

'There's something happening but I'll let you know if I get worried. But I like Leon too. I think despite an illusion of aloofness he's a man to be sure of in tough times. A man's man perhaps, but I've always thought you hadn't yet found a man you couldn't walk over. He could be one of those and I'm looking forward to the tussle with great anticipation.'

Tammy slanted a look at her. 'Not very motherly of you.'

Misty just smiled. 'You never wanted me to be your mother, Tam. I'm grateful to be your friend.'

Tammy felt the prickle of tears. Not something she did often and she impulsively hugged Misty. 'I'm the lucky one.' She stepped back and straightened. 'And I'm out of here. Jen's staying another night until Ken comes home— the truck broke down at Longreach.'

She picked up her bag. 'Trina's at home in early labour, and she missed her last two appointments while away in Brisbane, so I'm not sure of her baby's size. He was a little bigger than expected last time I saw her. She knows I'm concerned. She's ringing after five so let me know if you need a hand. I'm on call tonight. Have a good shift.'

'I understand Leon Bonmarito is visiting?' Misty's face was bland.

Tammy tilted her head. 'That was last night.'

'So it was.' Misty nodded with a smile. 'Enjoy your evening.'

CHAPTER FOUR

So Tammy wasn't surprised when the doorbell rang at nine-thirty that night. Nor was she surprised at the identity of the caller. 'Come in. I'm guessing Paulo's asleep.'

'And Louisa is watching over him. I am learning to trust he is safe again.' Leon's strong white teeth flashed in the low light. 'I would like to take Louisa home to Italy. Perhaps a change of scenery would be good for her. Do you think she'd come?'

'No.' Louisa had been housekeeper at the old doctor's residence, a short-term accommodation house for visiting doctors and nurses for a lot of years. Her husband had established Lyrebird Lake hospital and recently passed away.

'I'm sure my brother has suggested I stay at the residence and not at the resort because he wants me to fall in love with Louisa's cooking. And her stories. Has she told you about the myth of the lyrebird?'

Tammy had never been a fan of fairytales. 'I've heard of it. In all my years at the lake I've never seen one. Emma has, twice, once with your brother.' She smiled at how that ended. 'You'd better watch out.'

He, too, smiled. 'I think to see a bird will not change my life.'

'Louisa's husband used to say the lyrebird heals those in pain.' She had the feeling Leon could do with a spot of healing but it was none of her business.

She returned to the notion of Leon worrying about Louisa. 'Louisa spends time with her stepson's family.' She couldn't help but think it strangely endearing that this big, quiet man was concerned for an elderly widow he barely knew. She'd made a mental note to visit Louisa herself in case she needed more company. 'We won't let you steal her. We'd all miss her too much.'

She glanced at the clock. 'If you want a coffee, I'll offer you one now. I'm on call and I know one of the girls has come in to birth with Misty and there's another woman due out there.'

'Please, to the coffee.' He followed her when she stood and moved into the kitchen and she put her hand up to halt him at the door. He kept coming until his chest touched her fingers, a wicked glint in his eye that warned he didn't take orders easily either, but then he stopped.

She shifted her fingers quick-smart and tried not to recognise how good the warmth of his solid chest had felt beneath her palm. She needed at least three feet between them for her to breathe. 'If you can make my den feel small you'll crowd my kitchen. Just stay there and let me work.'

He lifted one brow but obediently leaned against the doorframe, relaxed but alert, and they were both aware he was capable of swift movement, if he wished.

She breathed out forcefully as she turned away. Thank goodness he'd stopped. The guy was too much of a man to ignore when he was this close and a powerful incentive to get her chore done quickly and move out of here.

Then he said quietly, as if the thought had just occurred to him, 'If you are called in to work, who is here for your Jack?' Was that censure in his voice? Disapproval?

It had better not be. Nobody disapproved of her mothering. She flicked him a glance and his face was serious. 'We have an intercom between the houses and I switch it on for my father to listen in. Jack knows he can call for his grandfather if I'm not around and Dad takes him next door.' She glared at him and pressed the button on the machine for espresso and the beans began to grind—like her teeth.

'And what if Ben is called out?' Still the frown when it was none of his business but then, suddenly, she remembered he'd had a recent fright himself. One she'd put her foot in at the wedding. She eased the tension that had crept into her neck.

Of course he'd be security conscious. She didn't need to be so quick to take offence. 'We don't do the same nights on call,' she explained. 'That's the beauty of a small town and friends who organise rosters between families.'

The aroma of fresh beans made her nose twitch with calmer thoughts and she forced herself to stay relaxed. The guy could make her nerves stretch taut like a rubber band ready to snap back and sting her.

He nodded and looked at her almost apologetically, as if aware he may have overstepped a boundary. 'I begin to see the sense of this place.'

To her further astonishment he smiled and added, 'Perhaps I am less surprised at my brother's decision to spend half his time here.'

She had the feeling that could've been a huge admission for him but she didn't pursue it. She didn't want him to think it mattered to her. It didn't. Really. Time for a subject change. The coffee spurted from the twin spouts and filled their cups and she turned with them in her hands to face him.

He didn't move initially and she realised her hands were full. He could touch her if he wished. She was defenceless. Something told her he realised it too. She lifted her brows at him and waited.

He grinned and heaved himself off the door-frame and stepped back to allow her past him into the den.

'See how I understand your look?'

She bit back her smile as she sat his coffee on the low table almost on top of another of those fundraising pamphlets. She shifted it and her eye was caught by the title.

"Wanted! Man Willing To Wax Chest For Fundraising."

She had a sudden image of Leon and the gurgle of laughter floated up like the brown bean froth in the cup.

'You find that funny?'

She shook her head and bit her lip. She handed him the flyer. 'Lucky you're not here for long.'

He looked down at the paper and grimaced. 'And a man would do this?'

She couldn't help her glance at his broad chest, a few dark hairs gathered at the neck. 'They haven't found a volunteer yet. Want to offer?'

'No.' He shook his head with a smile. 'Though—' he paused and eyed her '—it would depend on who is doing the waxing.' The look he sent her left no doubt there'd be a price paid for the privilege.

Tammy felt the heat start low down, potent and ready to flame, like a hot coal resting on tissue paper. Yikes. She snatched the flyer from him and stuffed it behind a cushion on the sofa. 'Do you have much to do with young babies in your hospital?'

He settled back with a hint of smile and left the topic, clearly amused by her pink cheeks. 'No. Neonatal surgery is too specialised and we don't have a neonatal intensive care. But perhaps we would need a special care nursery if the maternity wing went ahead.'

He leaned forward and she could tell he was weighing possibilities and scenarios. She could see the big businessman she'd mentally accused him of being before she'd known him better, before she'd been kissed by him perhaps. But she had no doubt that if such a venture could be successful, then Leon would be the man to do it.

'These are all things to be taken into consideration if we opened a midwifery service. I'm sure a lot has changed since my obstetric rotation a decade ago. At the moment of birth, I mean.'

She could talk about that all day—and night. 'You're right. Things have changed a lot.' She tried to imagine Leon as a young medical student, diffident and overawed like those she'd seen in her training, but he was too strong a personality for her to imagine him ever being daunted by setting. 'I think the biggest change here is to keep the baby with the mother at all times from the moment of birth. Not separate in a cot. With emphasis on skin-to-skin contact for the first hour at least. At birth, we try not to clamp the umbilical cord for a few minutes either, unless we really have to.'

He nodded with a little scepticism. 'If the baby requires resuscitation?'

'Sure.' She brushed the hair out of her eyes. 'Though not always. It's a little trickier but the latest studies have shown that not cutting the umbilical cord for at least three minutes after birth is beneficial, though perhaps not that long in resuscitation.'

His face said he couldn't see how that would work so she explained more. 'We can give oxygen and even cardiac massage on the bed with the mother and that allows us to keep the blood flow from the cord as well. We've had great success with it. But then all our babies that come through the centre are low risk so any problems they have at birth are usually transient and should be resolved fairly quickly.'

He looked unconvinced and she couldn't help teasing him. 'Or is this a little too radical for your maternity hospital idea?'

'I'm always willing to see and hear of new ideas.' He raised his eyebrows at her comment, so quick to respond to any negative feedback she gave him, but she had no time to go on before the phone rang.

She dug her mobile out of her pocket. It was Misty and she had to leave.

'Sorry. I'm needed in birthing. You'll have to go.' Leon's eyebrows rose haughtily and Tammy almost smiled. She could tell he wasn't used to that. A woman had to go and he would be left cooling his heels.

He stood, though to say he did it obediently didn't suit the way he complied. 'You are not in awe of me at all, are you, Tamara?'

She didn't have time for this, unfortunately. 'Should I be?' She switched on the intercom between the two houses. 'I hope I haven't jinxed us talking about resuscitation and healthy babies.'

She saw his mind switch to the medical urgency. 'What was said?'

She gave him half an ear as she scooped up her keys. 'On the phone? Misty's concerned at the delay in second stage, and there's some unease with the baby's heart rate,' she murmured as she closed the front door behind them both. 'If it was bad she'd ship them out to the base hospital, but backup is always good when the back of your neck prickles. Do you want to come?'

He shrugged. 'I'm not registered in this country but happy to advise you if needed. Please.'

'Fine. People know Gianni so they'll have no problem accepting your presence.'

He hesitated at the two cars. 'I'll meet you there. No sense leaving your car or mine here because we don't know how long you'll be.'

They met outside the hospital and she let them in through the side entrance. Trying to remain unobtrusive they drifted into the birthing room and over to Misty. The lighting was still dim but Tammy saw the heater on for the infant resuscitation trolley and the preparations Misty had made. And the birthing mother, Trina, was beside the bed and not in the bath.

There was even a flicker of relief in her step-mother's eyes when she saw Leon. Tammy's stomach tightened. With uncomplicated births the midwife called a staff member from another part of the hospital as an extra pair of hands. If the midwife was uneasy she called the on-call midwife or doctor as a more experienced backup.

Misty spoke quietly so as not to disturb the couple who were leaning over the bed together. 'Trina's been pushing for an hour and a half now and everyone's getting tired. There's good descent of the head but there's still a heck of a lot of baby to come.'

Tammy nodded. 'Do you want to transfer?'

Misty shook her head. 'Maybe earlier would have been better but Trina didn't want to go. We're just getting a head-on view now and we don't want a difficult birth lying down in an ambulance. Trina's done an amazing job.' She eased her neck stiffness. 'Thanks for coming.

I wanted some backup for the end. We'll move to all fours when the head's almost here.'

'Sure. Good call.' Tammy was peripherally aware that Leon had moved to the resuscitation trolley and was checking the drawers. Excellent. It would be much easier if he knew what they had and where it was. He shut the bottom drawer, glanced up and nodded.

She hoped they wouldn't need him.

The next pain came and the expulsive efforts from Trina were huge. Tammy could see why Misty was impressed with Trina's progress. Slowly a thatch of baby's hair could be seen and Misty helped Trina down onto her hands and knees, the position least likely to result in a baby's shoulder becoming lodged behind the pubic bone of the mother.

During the next contraction the baby's head was born. Tammy raised her eyebrows at Misty. Not a small head and the fact didn't auger well for small shoulders. Tammy glanced at the clock.

'If your baby's shoulders feel tight remember you can help by bringing your chest in close. Nipples to knees. That flattens the curve of your coccyx and allows baby an extra centimetre or two.' All calm and quiet instructions that Tammy knew Misty would have given before this stage as well.

As the seconds passed and they waited for the next contraction, the skin of the baby's scalp faded from pink to pale blue, and Tammy could feel her own heart rate begin to gallop as the handheld Doppler amplified the way Trina's baby's heart rate slowed. The contraction finally began again and baby's head seemed to try to extend but didn't move and Tammy crouched down beside Trina's ear. 'Bring your knees together as close as you can and flatten your breasts down towards your knees. You're doing awesome.'

Trina squashed down as much as she could and Misty supported the baby's head. The contraction built. 'Okay, Trina, push now.'

Trina pushed and suddenly her baby eased under the arch of her mother's pelvis and tumbled limply into Misty's hands. 'Flip around, Trina, so we can lay baby on your warm stomach and have a look at this little bruiser.'

Misty wiped the baby briskly with a warm towel and passed her baby, all cord and limbs and damp skin, back to Trina between her legs, and the new mother shifted around until she was lying on her back with her stunned baby flaccid on her stomach.

Misty used the little handheld Doppler directly against the baby's chest and the comparatively slow thump-thump-thump of the baby's heart rate made them all look at the clock.

'Over a hundred,' Leon said, 'and some re-spiratory effort.' He leaned down and held the green oxygen tubing near baby's face until the little body became gradually more pink.

'Thirty seconds since birth,' Tammy said, and as if on cue Trina's baby screwed her face up and began to cry in a gradually increasing volume. Except for the slight blueness in her face from the tight fit, Trina's baby was vigor-ous and pink all over now as she roared her disapproval of the cool air Leon was holding near her nose.

He took it away and watched Tammy and Misty exchange smiles, and Misty's shoulders dropped with relief. She slid the baby up Trina's body to her breasts and put a warm blanket over both of them.

'What do you think she weighs?' Trina's husband seemed to have missed the tenseness the attendants had felt and Misty wiped her forehead with the back of her wrist.

'I'd say at least eleven pounds.' She looked at Trina. 'What do you think, Trina?'

Trina looked away from her baby and grinned widely up at Misty. 'She's as big as a watermelon. And I'm stiff and sore but glad it's over. She's definitely my biggest—' she glanced at her husband '—and my last.'

'I'm glad you mentioned you don't cut the cord immediately,' Leon said quietly into Tammy's ear. 'Or I would have been expecting a different sequence of events.'

They'd moved back away from the birthing couple to the sink to strip off their gloves and wash their hands. Tammy nodded. 'Do you think it would have made much difference if we'd clamped and cut and moved the baby to the resuscitation trolley?'

'Not with an adequate heart rate like that.'

He paused and she wondered if he was comparing this with other occasions he'd known. 'Actually, no, and I can see advantages. It is always good to see differences in the way things are managed in other hospitals, let alone other countries.'

They waved to Misty and let themselves out. The parents were absorbed in their new daughter and waved absently.

Tammy smiled at the man walking beside her. 'It was good to know you were there. If those shoulders had been more stubborn we would have had a baby in much poorer condition, and in resuscitation the more hands the better.'

'The maternal positioning worked very well. My memories of shoulder dystocia were always fraught with a dread that was missing tonight.' He smiled. 'You were both remarkably calm.'

'There's some anxiety when you see a very large baby like Trina's. But we do drills for that scenario at least once a week so if there's a delay we can move straight into the positions. Because we knew Trina's baby was larger, Misty would have spoken to her about what to do if needed and good positions to try. But it can happen with small babies too.'

He dropped his arm around her shoulders, and it was companionable, not sexual. Not something she would have believed possible earlier. 'You must be very proud of your team here.'

'We are.' His arm felt warm and heavy but not a heaviness she wanted to shrug off. A heaviness of wanting to snuggle in and encourage more snuggling. She shifted away from that concept quick-smart and he picked up the tiny movement and slid his arm away. She pretended she didn't miss it. 'And the women and their families love the centre and the choice it gives them. We've quite a clientele from the larger centres coming here to birth and then going home from here.'

They were crossing the car park to Tammy's car and Tammy suddenly realised how at ease she felt with this big, quiet Italian. How she'd just expected that if Trina's baby had been compromised by a long delay before the rest of her body was able to be birthed, that Leon would be there to help. Despite his denial that he'd had much to do with new babies, she had unshakable conviction that his skills would be magnificent.

You can't tell that, a voice inside her insisted. But just like she knew that Misty could see things without proof or concrete evidence, she knew that Leon Bonmarito would be a great asset in Lyrebird Lake. Not that there was much chance of him hanging round.

She paused beside her car to speak and he took the opportunity to open her car door for her. She frowned. No one had done that for her for years and she wasn't sure she liked the warm and pampered feeling it left her with. As if abdicating her independence. But that uneasiness didn't stop her invitation. 'Perhaps I'll see you tomorrow night. If you find yourself at a loose end after Paulo's in bed.'

He inclined his head. 'Three in a row? What will people say?' At her arrested expression he laughed softly and looked around at the sleeping town. 'Your townspeople bed early, I doubt anyone is awake to notice.'

What would they notice? There was nothing to see. She'd done nothing wrong. Nobody could construe otherwise but it was as well he reminded her. She'd vowed to remain squeaky clean and the soul of discretion once she'd had Jack. Lyrebird Lake had given her tarnished youth a brand-new, shiny start, and there'd never been any hint of wayward behaviour to jeopardise that from Dr Ben's daughter.

She looked up at him, confident she'd done nothing wrong, nothing remotely possible to compromise her good name, and her chin lifted as she peered up at him in the dimness. Unexpectedly she perceived the unmistakable glint in those bedroom eyes of his. The breath caught in her throat and she moistened her lips to make the words, at the very least, sound relaxed. 'Notice what?'

'Perhaps this?' His hands came up and cupped both cheeks to prevent her escape, not with force but with warmth and gentleness and definite intent. His head bent and his chiselled lips met hers with an unmistakable purpose that spun her away from streetlights and neigh-bours and petty concerns of her good name, until she kissed him back because that was more natural than breathing, more satisfying than a heartfelt sigh, and kindled the smoulder of heat in her belly he'd started with a dance two days before.

When Leon stepped back she swayed until he cupped his hand on the point of her shoulder and held her steady.

Her hand lifted to her mouth of its own accord—suddenly sensitive lips tingled and sang—and she could feel the sleepiness in her eyes until she blinked it away. She glanced at the silent streets. The only lights shining were the street lamps. And no doubt her eyes.

Where had all these feelings come from? How could she feel so attuned and connected to this man she barely knew? How could she be tempted in a way she hadn't been since Jack was conceived? The depth of her response scared the pants off her. And she knew what had happened last time she'd felt like that.

He's right, she thought with convoluted logic,

this was dangerous, and she'd need to think what she was doing before she ended up as the latest discussion point at the local shop.

She moved back another step. 'I could see how people could form the wrong idea,' she said wryly, and then she swallowed a nervous laugh as she slipped past him into the car. She stared straight ahead as she turned the key. 'Thanks for the reminder and for being there for all of us tonight.' And for the kiss, but she wasn't saying that out loud.

As an exit line it wasn't bad. Showed she had presence of mind—something she wouldn't have bet on one minute ago. 'If you visit, maybe you could walk to my house tomorrow night, instead of driving. More discreet.'

As she drove away she decided the invitation had been very foolish. And not a little exciting. She was a sad case if that was how she got her thrills.

CHAPTER FIVE

LEON glanced in the oval hallway mirror beside the door and grimaced at the five-o'clock shadow that darkened his jaw. His watch said it was too late to shave again this evening. And no time to walk.

Paulo had been unsettled tonight and Leon doubted Tamara would appreciate a ten-o'clock visit. If he didn't know better he would say he was wary of upsetting her.

Little firebrand. He could feel the tilt of his mouth as he remembered the wedding and her not so veiled threats of violence to his person. And the kiss last night under the street lamp. That had been bad of him. The man in the mirror smiled. Not that he wouldn't do it again if he had the chance. The result had far exceeded his wildest expectations and the ramifications had disturbed his slumber again for much of the night. It was fortunate he'd never required much sleep.

She amused him, intrigued him, but most of all she burned his skin with Vesuvian fire whenever he touched her and that should be enough to warn him off. He couldn't deny the danger but then she was so different than the women he was used to.

There was no fawning or attempts to use guile. He laughed out loud as his hired car ate up the short distance to her house—she did not know the meaning of the word *subtlety*.

Though no doubt she'd prefer he walked and with less fanfare of his arrival, and he needed to remind himself this town was different to Rome. Even Gianni had told him that. Perhaps he would walk tomorrow if he was invited again.

Another smile twitched at his lips. That would be two days before they left and each day he was becoming more interested in the concept of his new sister-in-law bringing her friend to visit his homeland.

When he knocked quietly on the door, it wasn't Tamara who opened the door, but her father, Ben, with his grandson standing behind his back. The degree of Leon's disappointment was a stern warning of how quickly he was becoming accustomed to Tamara's company.

'Evening, Leon. Tammy said you might call. She's over in the birthing unit with Misty.'

Another crisis? 'Do they need a hand?'

Ben shrugged but there was tension in his smile. 'Haven't asked for one but you could hang around outside on standby. Misty said it was good having you there last night. Or you could wait with us?'

'Perhaps I will return to the hospital and check. It will be too late for visitors when she's finished anyway.'

'I'll give her a quick ring and let her know you're available, then.'

'Thank you.' He nodded at Ben and turned away. He could hear Tammy's son asking why he had come. Perhaps a question he should be asking himself. But at the moment he was more interested in his instinct that he be there in case Tamara needed him.

Leon had intended to poke his head into the birthing room and then wait at the nurses' station until he heard the sound of a well baby. What he did hear when he arrived was the sound of the suction and oxygen and the murmur of concerned voices. When he opened the door his eyes caught Tammy's and the urgent beckon of her head had him beside her before he realised he'd moved.

'Will you tube this little guy, please, so we can have a look? He's not responding as well as I'd like.' She had the equipment ready to hand him, the laryngoscope, the endotracheal tube and introducer, even the tape. 'I thought I was going to have to do it myself but I'd rather you did.'

Easily, but that would not help her next time. 'Then go with that thought. You do it and I'll help. Better for when I am not here.' She swallowed and nodded and he tapped the dispenser of hand cleaner on the side of the trolley and quickly cleaned his hands before handing the laryngoscope to her.

'No rush,' he said conversationally, and steadied her hand with his as she fumbled a little. 'His colour is adequate so your resuscitation has maintained his oxygen saturation but a direct vision and an airway into his lungs is a good idea if he's not responding.'

He handed Tammy the equipment in order as she gently tilted the baby's head into the sniffing position as she'd been taught, and viewed the cords with the laryngoscope.

Misty murmured background information to fill Leon in. 'A true knot in his very short umbilical cord and it must have pulled tight as he came down.' They all glanced at the manual timer on the resuscitation trolley as the second hand came around to the twelve. 'So quite stunned at birth. Heart rate's been sixty between cardiac massage, and he's two minutes old. We've been doing intermittent positive pressure since birth and cardiac massage since thirty seconds. He's slow to respond.'

Tammy passed the suction tube once when the laryngoscope light bulb illuminated a tenacious globule of blood that must have occluded half of the baby's lungs from air entry.

'That will help,' she murmured. This time when they connected the oxygen to the ET tube she slid down his throat, his little chest rose and fell and his skin quickly became pink all over.

'Heart rate one hundred,' Misty said when she ceased the chest compressions to count, and they all stood back as the baby began to flex, wince and finally attempted to cry around the tube in his throat.

'I love the way all babies wish to live,' Leon murmured. 'It is their strength.' He nodded at Tammy and gestured with his hand. 'Slide the tube out. He doesn't need it now.' He felt the pride of her accomplishment expand in his chest and smiled at her as the little boy began to wail his displeasure. 'Well done.' He nodded his approval of her skill. 'How did that feel?'

Tammy's voice had the slightest tremor that matched the one in her fingers now it was all over. 'Better now I've done it again. Thanks.'

Misty lifted the crying babe and carried him back to his mother, who sat rigidly up in the bed with her empty arms outstretched to take him.

Tears ran down her face and even her husband wiped his eyes as their baby cried and the mountain of fear gradually faded from their eyes like dye from new denim.

'Don't do that to Mummy, Pip,' the dad said as his wife's arms closed over her baby and she hugged him to her chest. Her husband's arms came around them both and their heads meshed together in solidarity. The baby blinked and finally settled to squint at his parents through swollen eyelids.

The dad looked across at Misty. 'He'll be all right, won't he, Misty?'

'He's good, Trent.' She glanced at Tammy and Leon to include them. 'A clot of blood was stuck in his throat. We'll watch him for the next twenty-four hours but Pip responded well once the airway was clear. No reason to think otherwise.'

'That was terrifying,' the mother said with a catch in her voice.

Leon smiled. 'Yes. Always. Of course this is the beginning of many frights this child will give you.' He smiled again. 'I know. I have a son.' He bent and listened with the stethoscope to the baby's little chest. 'Your son sounds strong and healthy, and obviously he was born under a lucky star.'

His mother shivered. 'How's that lucky?'

'A true knot in the umbilical cord is dicing with danger. The knot could have pulled tight much earlier when there was nothing we could do but he waited until it was safe to do so. And in such a good place as this.'

Misty and Tammy smiled and the parents looked at each other as if to say, Thank goodness we have a clever child.

'If you excuse me, I'll leave you to enjoy your family.' He leaned across and shook the father's hand, nodded at the mother and smiled at Misty.

'I'm ready to come with you,' Tammy said as she glanced at Misty for confirmation.

'Go. I'm fine. Thanks again. Both of you.'

They left, shutting the door behind them, and when they reached the outside, Tammy inhaled the night air deep into her lungs and let it out as if her very breath had been hung with lead weights. 'I hate that floppiness in a compromised infant.' She shuddered with relief.

He could see that. Clearly. 'Of course. Everyone does. You did well,' Leon said quietly at her shoulder, and to his surprise he realised she was wiping at tears. Instinctively he pulled her gently into his chest and held her safe against him with her nose buried in his shirt. This time only for comfort and he was surprised how good it felt to be able to offer this.

But Tamara in his arms was becoming a habit. She felt warm and soft and incredibly precious within his embrace and the fragrance of her filled his head. His hand lifted and stroked her hair, hair like the softest silk, and the bones of her skull under his fingers already seemed familiar. He accepted he would find her scent on his skin when she was gone. Like last night. And the night before. And the night before that. The thought was bittersweet. 'You did beautifully.'

Her head denied his approval and her voice was muffled by his shirt. 'I should have done it earlier.'

'You could not know there was an obstruction there. To decide to intubate is no easy decision. And the time frame was perfect because he was well perfused while the decision was made.'

She unburrowed her head from his chest. Obviously she'd just realised she was in his arms again and wondering how that happened. He couldn't help the twitch of his lips.

'This is becoming a bit of a habit.' She said it before he could.

'Hmm. So it is.' He could hear the smile in his voice as she stepped back.

'I'll be more confident next time.' There was no amusement to spare in hers. His arms felt empty, like the mother must have felt before she was given her baby, but he felt anything but maternal towards Tamara. Probably better that she stepped away because his thoughts had turned from mutual comfort to mutual excitement in a less public place.

He forced himself to concentrate on her concerns. 'Do not disparage yourself. I'm impressed. Intubation is a skill that not all midwives have and very useful for unexpected moments. It was very brave of you to conquer your fears.'

She straightened and met his eyes. 'I felt better once I knew you were there as backup.'

He was glad he could help. The streetlight illuminated the delicate planes of her face, the shadows lengthened her already ridiculously long neck and his fingers tensed inside his pocket where he'd sent them to hide because he itched to cup her jaw. Already his mouth could imagine the taste of her, the glide of his mouth along that curve that beckoned like a siren, but a siren unaware of her power. He drew a low breath and looked away. 'I'm glad I was there.'

'So am I.' He felt she avoided his eyes this time and maybe it was better. 'I should get home to Dad and Jack. They'll be worried.'

He wasn't sure either of them would be worried but he could tell she was uncomfortable and maybe a little aware of the danger she was in. Her night had been stressful enough without him adding pressure. 'And I will see you tomorrow. Sleep well, Tamara.' He wouldn't.

'Tammy,' she corrected automatically. And then she smiled. 'Goodnight, Leonardo.' He liked the sound of his name on her lips.

The next afternoon Tammy and Misty stood beside Pip's wheeled cot and stared down at him as he slept. 'Lucky little guy.'

Misty shook her head. 'It's always when you least expect it. The labour was perfect, Pip's heart rate all the way was great, and then I just started to feel bad, edgy for no reason, and I had to call you.'

Tammy gave a quick squeeze of her step-mother's arm for comfort. 'Your instinct has always been terrific.'

Misty rolled her eyes. 'I did wonder if Trina's birth from the night before had given me the willies and I was losing my nerve. You know, doubting myself by wanting to call you.' She looked at Tammy. 'You were great. I'm really pleased you came.'

'Your turn to intubate next time. I'm pleased that Leon came as well. I know that if we do what we did, just keeping the oxygen and cir-culation going until they recover, we're going to be fine. I *know* babies want to live.'

They stared down at Pip and Tammy went on. Voicing what they both knew. 'The hor-rible thing is that every now and then, for their own reasons, babies don't do what we expect. On that day I want to know we did everything we could. Maybe we could ask Leon about the latest resuscitation techniques before he leaves?'

Misty nodded. 'I think everyone would be interested in a discussion and the practise too. I know your father would. We need to include it more, like we practise the emergency drills.'

That was the beauty of working at Lyrebird Lake. Everyone wanted to keep their skills top notch. Wanted to support growth and competency and faith in one another. 'We need to include new trends in Resus more.'

'Next time I see him I'll ask him.' Probably tonight, she thought with a bubbling anticipation she tried to ignore. 'It'll have to be soon because he'll be gone.' She hoped she didn't sound plaintive.

Misty missed nothing. 'Sunday, isn't it? I think you'll miss him. You okay with that?'

Tammy reached for a pile of nappies to re-stock Pip's cot. At least she could avoid Misty's eyes that way. 'Fine. No problem.' She didn't want to think about it. Something she hadn't been able to achieve in reality. She shrugged. 'I've enjoyed his company, but really, we barely know each other.'

And yet on another level they knew each other far too well.

Misty might have been able to read her mind but there was no pressure in her comment. 'Sometimes it doesn't take long to feel that connection.'

Tammy smiled at the pile of nappies. 'Like you did with Dad?'

She could hear the returning smile in Misty's voice. 'I can remember driving away as I tried to deny it.'

She'd heard the story many times and never tired of it. 'And he followed you to Lyrebird Lake.' Tammy stood and glanced over at her stepmother. 'I'm glad he did, and glad he brought me with him. But I can't see Leon hanging around here for me and I'm certainly not moving to Italy.'

She thought about the differences in their cultures and she thought about distance and all she'd achieved here. Then she thought about her bad run with Italians and finally the kidnap attempt on Leon's son, even though the criminals had been caught and Paulo was safe now. She couldn't imagine living a life like that.

Misty handed her some clean singlets to put under the cot. 'I'm sure your father told me once you can speak Italian?'

She didn't know why she wanted to hug that to herself. 'Only a little.'

'Does Leon know?' Tammy shook her head.

Misty smiled. 'Isn't that interesting.' She moved away from Pip's bed to change the subject. 'I'm actually glad it's my last evening tonight. Peta and Nicky want to go to the beach house on the weekend and your father says he's not going without me. It'll be good to relax.'

Tammy thought of her father and the runaround her stepsisters would give him if Misty wasn't there to gently control their exuberance. 'I don't blame him. The girls are full-on.'

Misty laughed. 'And Jack isn't?'

'Must be in the genes.' They smiled at the family joke. Though Ben wasn't Tammy's biological father they'd decided Tammy had inherited all her bad traits from him.

'Actually—' Misty paused as if weighing her words '—I was wondering if Jack would like to come with us? Give you a weekend off.'

Tammy frowned at the sudden unease the thought left her with. All this talk of kidnapping and violence and her son away. Then she thought of her response when she'd thought Leon was coddling his own son. 'Maybe not this weekend. But another time, sure. As long as I can take the three of them some weekend and you and Dad could have a weekend off?'

'We could do that.' Misty glanced at the clock and saw it was almost time for Tammy to go. 'Has Jack been keeping Paulo company?'

She'd tried to encourage her son to visit but he'd resisted. 'Not yet. I'm not sure they get on. I have a feeling they both like being only children. Rivalry. I'm taking him around to Louisa's this afternoon to play.'

Tammy glanced at her watch. 'Did you want to send the girls around after school? Louisa would love it. The more children, the happier she is. Just until Dad gets home with Leon?

I'll be there too.' Not to mention she'd be there when Leon came home. She wouldn't have to wait until late that night to see him and the thought sat warmly just under her throat.

Misty glanced at her own watch and weighed up the time she had to change plans. 'Instead of after-school care? They'd like that.'

'It was Louisa's idea for the children to visit.' And Tammy had been quick to agree. 'I've been meaning to catch up with her for a few days.'

Misty nodded as they both paused and thought about Louisa's loss and Tammy went on. 'Leon says she's lonely. That the residence is too big and empty for her.'

Misty bit her lip. 'Poor Louisa. Maybe she needs a change of scenery to help her think of something else for a while?'

'Leon says he's trying to get her to move to Italy with him.' She was starting all her sentences with 'Leon says.' Good grief. She needed to watch that and she'd bet her step-mama wouldn't miss it either. She changed the subject. 'I wonder where Gianni took Emma for the Australian leg of their honeymoon?'

Tammy saw Misty bite back her smile as she accepted the change. 'She'll send us a postcard, I'm guessing. It's not long till they fly out.'

Tammy glanced at her watch. It was time for her to go before she said something else she'd regret. 'Yep. Imagine—Italy on Sunday.' She didn't look at Misty as she left. Just waved and stared straight ahead.

'I don't want to play with him. I'm not a little kid, Mum, you can't make me.' Tammy glanced across and checked that Jack had done up his seatbelt before she started the car. Stinky pulled against his dog restraint and panted longingly at the window.

'Sure I can.' She ruffled Jack's black hair. 'So stop acting like a baby and be nice. The girls are coming too. The poor kid's probably bored out of his skull not being able to go to school.'

Jack screwed up his nose. 'Poor Paulo. Imagine not having to go to school? How terrible.'

'Don't be sarcastic. It doesn't suit you.' Tammy tried to keep a straight face. There was a lot of muttering going on under Jack's breath and she thought she heard, 'I'd kill to not have to go to school.' She could remember thinking the same thing a lot of years ago.

She parked outside and walked the path of the old doctor's residence and up the stairs onto the verandah. Tammy knocked and opened the door. The residence was always open and Louisa would be out the back in the kitchen.

The tantalising aroma of fresh baking wafted

down the hallway and she sighed philosophically about her new jeans that were a little tight already. Louisa's scones were legendary.

'Hello, Jack.' Tiny Louisa held out her snuggly-grandma arms and smiled hugely as she enveloped him in a big hug. Louisa was the only person he'd suffer a hug from and the sight made Tammy smile too.

Jack emerged pink cheeked, grinned shyly, and he leaned up and kissed Louisa's cheek. 'Hello, Aunty Lou.'

'You need fattening up, my boy. You and Paulo are like two skinny peas in a pod.' She glanced fondly over at Paulo, who sat beside the window with an open book in front of him. 'Paulo's been forcing down my scones. Haven't you, Paulo?'

Paulo smiled shyly at Louisa and kissed his fingers. *'Delizioso.'*

Tammy stepped in for her own hug, and

she squeezed Louisa's waist which suddenly seemed smaller than she remembered. She frowned. 'You losing weight, Louisa?'

Louisa patted her round tummy. 'Oh, I'm not cooking as much, though I've put on a pound or three since two more gorgeous Italians moved in.'

Tammy felt slightly reassured but decided she'd mention Louisa's health to her dad next time she saw him.

She noticed Jack had wolfed down his scones by the time Peta and Nicola arrived. Misty and Ben's girls were both fair-headed like their mother and Nicola stood half a head taller than her sister.

More hugs and more homemade strawberry jam and freshly whipped cream to be piled onto disappearing scones and then the children all trooped off to play outside. Tammy felt

Paulo dragged his feet a little and she frowned after him.

She glanced at Louisa. 'Maybe I should ring Montana? Paulo seemed happiest talking to Grace at the wedding.' Grace was staying with Montana and Andy's daughter while Gianni and Emma were on their first few nights of the honeymoon.

Louisa laughed. 'She'll be here soon. She and Dawn have been over every afternoon after school. The three get on very well.'

Tammy nodded, and helped Louisa carry their tea to the verandah. The women sat looking out over the green lawns, talked together easily while the children played and drank tea.

The sun shone on the red roof of the hospital across the road and fluffy white clouds made magical shapes in the blue of the sky. The breeze from the lake helped keep the temperature down and Tammy decided the two boys seemed to be getting on well enough.

The children's games started simply, though even to a casual observer the boys competed for most stakes. They always seemed to be the last two to be found in hide-and-seek and were the fastest at finding people. Both were better than the girls at shooting hoops and it quickly became apparent how important it was to be the boy with the best score. Tammy shook her head as Jack whooped when he won the latest game.

The afternoon sun sank lower and Louisa went back inside to start dinner while Tammy flicked through a magazine as she watched them play.

Leon would be home soon, and her thoughts returned to the man who had erupted into her life with a compelling force she wasn't prepared for.

She'd already seen his concern for Louisa but what was he like while he stayed here? Was he tidy and thoughtful? Did he wait to be served his meals or jump up to help? Was he a good father, attending to all Paulo's needs? At the last thought she pulled herself up. It didn't matter what the answer was to any of these questions, he was leaving on Sunday. And she was not going to waste her time wondering about things that didn't concern her.

She called out to the children to suggest they finish off their games and come in. Stinky barked as he tried to join in and the sound echoed over the quiet, tree-lined street.

Tammy glanced at her watch again. He'd be here soon. The questions she'd asked herself itched like a raised rash at the back of her mind and she gave in to the urge to search out Louisa for some of the answers before it was too late.

Her mind wandered to whether or not Leon would visit her house tonight as well.

Wandered to the night after he left for his home country and how empty her den would feel.

Wandered to whether the tension she could feel heating between them could be contained to prevent an inferno, a conflagration that could damage them both as they went their separate ways in the very near future.

Her hip buzzed and she reached for her phone. It was Misty and she opened it with a smile.

Her smile fell at the unease plain in her step-mother's voice. 'I've got a bad feeling.' Misty sounded shaky and Tammy felt her stomach drop. Misty went on. 'Where's your car?'

Tammy frowned into the phone. 'Outside. Why?'

'I'm coming over.' Misty hung up.

* * *

Outside, the girls were happy to quit but the boys had one more point they wanted to settle and the ultimate test was Jack's idea.

'Just one last race. A longer one. I'll race you past the last tree and around that car down the end of the road and back. No stopping.'

Paulo looked at the distance, pondering the slight incline in the hill over the rough stones and the fact that they both had bare feet. He'd always run well in bare feet. And he was fast.

'*Sì*. Then we must go in, for my father will be here soon.'

'You're on.' Jack looked at the girls. 'Grace? You be starter.'

Paulo looked confused and Grace whispered, 'I say, "Ready, set, go." On "go" you run like the clappers.'

Paulo nodded. He understood 'go'.

The other girls were silent as Grace counted. 'Ready. Set. Go.' The two boys took off like deer in the bush, along the path, down the hill, and Stinky ran with them, barking the whole way. The girls cheered as the two distant figures ran neck and neck and then split each side of the car as they came to it and turned for the return journey. Then a strange thing happened.

The car doors opened wide and two men got out and suddenly the boys disappeared. Almost as if they were sucked into the vehicle. Both of them. The doors shut and the car pulled away on the road out of town in a skid of gravel and the roar of an engine even the girls could hear.

All that was left was the dust and the tiny four-legged figure of Stinky chasing the black sedan down the road.

Grace blinked and looked at Nicky and Peta and then she spun on her heel and raced into the house. 'Tammyyyyy. Someone's taken them!'

* * *

Grace ran full pelt into Tammy, who'd just shut her phone and was staring at it as if trying to understand. She steadied the girl against her chest. When she realised Grace was crying, dread curled like a huge claw in her chest and she looked at the empty lawn. Where were the boys?

She thrust Grace aside into Louisa's arms and rushed out into the street. A white car backed out of a driveway down the road and drove away; otherwise, the road was deserted in every direction. No Jack. No Paulo. Just Nicky and Peta with their arms around each other in fright outside the door.

Tammy spun on her heel. 'Who took them, Grace?' Her brain searched for a reason. More kidnappers? 'What did they look like? It wasn't a white car, was it? What were they driving?'

Grace sniffed valiantly and her mouth opened and closed helplessly. Louisa hugged the little girl into her side as the older woman, too, tried to make sense of what had happened.

Grace swallowed a sob that blocked her throat. 'It was a black car.' She sniffed hugely and then the words tumbled out. 'It was parked down the road. The boys had a race and, when they ran past, men came out of the car and pushed them inside and drove off. Stinky's run after them.'

Tammy grabbed the keys to her own car off the table. 'Mind the kids, Louisa. I'm going after them.'

'Is that wise?' Louisa's vice trembled. 'It could be dangerous.'

'Dangerous for them,' Tammy snarled. 'Ring Dad to find Leon. Let Leon ring the police if he wants to.' Tammy was having trouble seeing through the thick fear in her head. How dare they take her son? And Leon's.

'They had black shirts and black trousers on,' Nicky said suddenly.

'And it was a car like Grandpa's,' Peta added.

Tammy's brain was chanting Jack's words over and over. *You'd find me, wouldn't you, Mum?*

Peta's words sank in as she threw her bag over her shoulder. 'A Range Rover?'

Peta nodded. 'Sort of. A big black four-wheel drive.'

'Right, then.' And Tammy was gone, running for her car and roaring away from the kerb as she fumbled with her seatbelt. They probably only had about three minutes head start on her and she knew the road. Misty's phone call came back to her. 'Where's your car?' And here she was in her car. She hoped to hell that Misty's premonition had seen a good end to the scenario.

The winding road into Lyrebird Lake could be treacherous for those who didn't know it. But then if they were Italians as she expected they were, they'd be used to driving on treacherous winding roads. Damn them. She pushed the pedal down harder and she flew past a gliding Maserati she barely recognised coming into town. A minute later her mobile phone rang and she snatched it up and didn't even consider it unusual she knew who it was. 'I can't drive and talk.'

'Put it on speaker.' Leon's order was calm, yet brooked no refusal. She flicked the speaker on impatiently and his voice echoed in the cabin. 'Stop your car, Tamara. Do not chase these people.'

Her foot lifted off the accelerator and then pushed down again. 'No. I won't stop.' She hung up and pushed the pedal down harder.

And nearly ran over Stinky, who appeared as she rounded a bend.

She skidded to a halt, reversed, leaned over to the passenger's side and opened the door. She breathed deeply in and out several times. She wasn't surprised when she looked in the rearview mirror and Leon's car was behind her.

Stinky's tongue was hanging twice its length as he gulped air. 'Get in, Stinky.' Stinky leaned his paws on the frame and sighed. Such was his dedication to chasing the boys he didn't have the energy left to jump in.

Tammy pulled on the handbrake, opened her door, dashed around the car and picked up the little dog, but before she could bundle him in, Leon pulled up behind her. He was out of his car in a flash.

'Do not follow them. That's an order. You do

not understand and will cause more harm than help.'

His words dashed over her like a bucket of cold water and she didn't reply as he went on implacably. 'Your son will be safer if you do not confront them.' His voice lowered. 'And so will mine.'

Her footsteps stopped beside her car, as did the frozen focus that had consumed her, and she slumped, horrified again at what had happened and chillingly aware of how the fear in her chest was almost choking her. She turned and leaned her face on her arm against the roof of her vehicle and then she felt Leon's hands as he pulled her back into his body.

She almost sank into him until she remembered he'd brought this on her. They'd taken Paulo and now he'd brought this agony to her when they'd taken Jack too. He wrapped his arms around her stiff body, but there was no yielding, no relief he could give her. Nothing would help the cold that seeped into her as if she were being slowly submerged in an icy blanket of dread. Her son had been abducted.

Her chest ached with the spiralling fear started by Misty's call and the empty yard.

And they sped away further as she stood here. She yanked herself free of his embrace. He was letting them get away. 'I could have caught them.' She threw her head back and glared into his face. 'Seen where they went.'

His voice was flat. Cold. Implacable. A stranger. 'I will know where they went. Those who follow them are better prepared to apprehend than you or me. I told you I had people protecting my family.'

Great. That was just great. 'And what about mine? Whose protection does my son have?'

'My protection too, of course,' he ground out. Her eyes flashed a deep fear at him that tore at his faith in his men and his belief he'd done the right thing to stop her. He'd done this to her. Why had he left Paulo again today? He'd created a pattern. The first rule of prevention. So much for his belief the threat had passed. So much for his efforts to not be too protective of his son. Now his nightmare had spilled over onto Tamara.

But he hadn't believed they'd follow him here. It didn't make sense. Why would they do such a thing? Was it not easier to wait until he returned to Italy? Even Gianni had thought danger in Australia highly unlikely. But thinking these thoughts brought no solace at this point.

She was waiting for a crumb of reassurance and he was too slow with it. 'Of course he will be safe. You have to trust me.'

She stepped back, further out of his arms, and spun away. 'You're asking a lot,' she threw over her shoulder as she paced. 'To trust you with the most important person to me in the world.'

He knew it was such a huge thing she entrusted to him. Her shoulders were rigid with it. 'I know,' he said.

She narrowed her eyes as she turned to face him. With her arms crossed tight across her breasts as if to hold in the fear, she searched for a hint of unsureness or ambivalence on the rightness of his actions. He hoped there was none.

Did she trust him? It was achingly important she could. Her chest rose and fell in a painful rasping breath full of unshed tears that tore at his own pain like the claws of a bird.

He saw the moment she accepted there was nothing physical she could do. He'd taken that away from her but he'd had to, for her own safety, and for the boys. She sagged back against her car. 'What happens now, then?'

'We go back home and wait.'

She shook her head angrily at the passiveness of the action, then threw herself off the car and back into action. 'I'm going to see Misty.'

CHAPTER SIX

'My mum's going to rip your arms off!'

'And my father will see you in hell.'

Both boys looked at each other and nodded. The captors, three dark-clothed Italian men, laughed as they drove.

Jack screwed up his face at the men and patted Paulo's leg. 'Don't worry, Paulo. She'll come.'

Paulo hunched his shoulders. 'It is my father who will come. And these dogs will pay.' The bravado was wearing a little thin but it still helped the fear that crept up their arms and settled around their tight little bellies as they sat wedged between two burly men. Two small boys in a situation they shouldn't have had to deal with.

'How have we two of them?' The Italian accent was coarser than Paulo's dad's and his partner shrugged.

'Didn't know which to take. We can get rid of the other one.'

In the back the boys huddled closer together.

Tammy parked her car outside Louisa's house and left the door gaping as she ran straight into Misty's arms. Ben came out of the house to meet them.

Leon heard Misty say, 'I feel they're fine. Honestly,' and he grimaced at the strange comment. He passed Tammy's open car door and shut it with tightly leashed control before he followed her in.

He felt suspended above himself, detached

and icy cold as though he were peering down a long tunnel when all he wanted to do was find the people who had taken their sons and crush their throats. But he needed to stay calm for Tamara—and for the boys. He'd been speaking to his bodyguards and they had caught up with the car but were keeping distance between them. They had to find a way to stop the vehicle and keep the boys safe.

When he entered the residence it seemed the room was full of people. Louisa, her lined face white and shaking, stared at him as if she didn't understand. Kidnappings and violence were not in her life and Leon moved swiftly across and folded her in his arms. He stroked her hair. Nothing like this would have ever happened before in Lyrebird Lake.

Leon remembered his hope he wouldn't need to call on his brother's help for just such a situation. Gianni wasn't here but it seemed he'd get as many people as he needed. But for the moment he had to trust his own men and, now that he'd just contacted them, the Australian police. They would ring him if he could do anything.

And past his fear for his son was Tammy, and her son's kidnapping, leaving Leon devastated he'd brought this on her by association, and regretful of her pain. His own agony was like a gaping wound in his chest and no doubt it would be as bad if not worse for a mother. Louisa shuddered in his arms and he rested his chin on the top of her grey head. Poor Louisa. Poor Tammy. And what of the boys?

The afternoon stretched into evening and then to night. Six hours after his return to the lake Leon stood tall and isolated in Tammy's den. He searched her face for ways to help but he knew she wasn't able to let herself relax enough to take the comfort he wanted to offer.

He carried the coffee he'd made her from the machine in the kitchen and the strong aroma of the familiar beans made him think of home. At home he would have more access to resources.

His arms ached to pull her against him and transfuse the strength she needed in the closing of this tumultuous day. Her distress left him powerless in a way he wasn't used to and he placed the cup on the mantel, then sighed as he reluctantly lowered himself to the sofa to watch her. 'I stay until we have them back.'

Tammy heard him. The coffee aroma drifted past her nose. She was glad he'd finally sat down. It gave her more room to pace and her eyes closed as she processed his words. *Until we have them back.* 'I want my son.' She wanted to wring her hands. 'I want Jack now. I don't want you.'

That wasn't strictly true. She'd driven everyone else away—her father, her stepmother—but she'd been unable to evict Leon from her presence. He'd flatly refused to leave her. And she needed him near her so she could know she was kept in the loop. Despite her wall of pain she seemed to be able to draw some strength from Leon which seemed absurd when he was the reason she was going through this.

She reached for the cup and took a sip. It was strong, and black, as she liked it. She'd drunk her coffee that way since she'd been that impressionable teen who'd fallen for a man similar to this one. Or was that unfair to Leon?

What was it with her and men that attracted trouble and danger?

At sixteen Vincente Salvatore had taught her to love his language, his country, all things

Italian, with a heady persistence that endeared her to him. An Italian with trouble riding his shoulders, hot-headed and hot-blooded. Then he blew it all away with a reckless abandon for right and wrong that left her with the realisation of just how dangerous his lifestyle was. She swallowed a half-sob in a gulp of coffee. Maybe Vincente's friends could find Jack.

How on earth had she embroiled herself and her son in trouble without realising it? But she would have to deal with that. It was her fault. She couldn't believe she'd been so irresponsible as to let the children out of her sight. Couldn't forgive herself for daydreaming her way to negligence. Such stupidity could have cost Jack his life. And Paulo his.

It wasn't as if she hadn't known of the possibility of danger. Even though Leon had said it was past. And what had she been doing? Daydreaming about a man. Following Louisa for titbits of gossip about his presence at the old residence. Anything to feed her growing fascination for Leon.

Well, it would all stop. Now. She would promise anyone who would listen that the risk of danger to her family far outweighed any fleeting attraction this dark Italian held over her.

A bargain.

Jack and Paulo back safe and she'd never think of the man again. Honest.

She should have learned that she was destined to be brought down by her heart, and the menace of these Mediterranean men, her nemeses. Now their sons had paid the price.

Unfortunately, at this moment, it was hard to keep those thoughts clear in her mind because her shattered emotions were torn—torn between guilt for her negligence, spiralling fear for the outcome and the gnawing need for comfort from the very man who caused it all.

Louisa had been gathered up from the residence by her stepson and whisked away. And Leon was here, the only barrier to the emptiness of this house.

It was eerie how she could imagine the outside of her empty house, dark and forlorn in the moonlight, and she glanced out the window to the shifting shadows in the street outside. Strained her ears for imagined sounds and then turned abruptly from the window and put the cup down.

She even ran her fingertips along the mantelpiece as if to catch dust and at least do something useful. Her mind was fractured into so many fear-filled compartments and what-ifs she couldn't settle.

She wanted both boys asleep in Jack's room, with Stinky's head on his paws as he watched his master—glancing at her every time she went in as if to ask if he could stay.

But the blue room at the end of the hall stayed empty like an unused shrine.

And Leon watched her.

It had taken until midnight for Tammy to decide she couldn't stay at her father's house. She'd said she wanted to be near Jack's things. Leon had refused to allow her to go alone and he was still glad he'd come. But as he watched her, she glittered like glass in moonlight with nervous energy. Every sound made her jump, every creak of the polished floorboards made her shiver, and Leon ached for the damage he'd caused to this sleepy town and to this woman.

He patted the sofa beside him and held out his hand. 'Come. Sit by me. Let me help you rest for a few moments at least.'

She turned jerkily towards him. 'I can't

believe he's not here.' Staccato words stabbed the air in the room like little knives, tiny steel-tipped blades of guilt that found their mark on him.

'They will have them by morning. My men have promised me.' Leon rose to slide his arm around her stiff shoulders and pull her down to sit beside him so their hips touched. She was so cold and stiff and he nudged more firmly against her hip, offering comfort to both of them, and a safe place to rest if only for a moment, and if only she could.

'Your men?' She sniffed. 'If they were so good the boys would never have been taken at all.'

'Nobody expected this here. We were lucky they were still with us.' Leon had his own demons. Paulo gone and he didn't know if he was alive. Or Jack. Surely they would get them back.

There had been no demand yet. Would they discard the boy they didn't need? Would they leave him alive? It had been his choice to delay the police while his men followed the trail initially.

The trail Tamara had wanted to chase. His first sight of her face as she drove past him like a woman possessed still affected him. Her little car pushed to its limits to the point where his more powerful motor could barely catch her. His throat tightened. 'I can't believe you pursued them in your car.'

She brushed the hair out of her eyes impatiently. 'Why would I not?' Her eyes searched his. 'I could still be chasing them if you hadn't stopped me. What if they've disappeared and we never find where they went? What, then?'

He shook his head at the thought. No! It would not be like that. He had to trust what his operatives told him. Tomorrow in the early morning, it would be okay. 'I was terrified for you as well. What were you going to do if you caught them?'

Her eyes burned. 'Whatever I had to. They have my son.'

And mine. She had no idea. And he did and should never have brought this on these people. He knew what loss and guilt did to people. 'What you did was too dangerous.'

Another swift scornful search of his face. 'For them?'

'For you and for the boys.'

She shook her head. 'For the first time in a lot of years I don't know what to do. You tell me to wait. But how long must I wait? I want him now.' Her shoulders slumped and slowly, like the deflation of an overstretched balloon, all the fight leaked out of her and she sagged against him as she buried her face in his shoulder.

He smoothed her hair. Had to touch her and try to soothe her agitation as she went on. 'There's never been such hard waiting. I've never had such fear. Make me forget the horror I can't shake. Talk to me. Tell me something that helps.'

He pulled her onto his lap and hugged her, still smoothing her hair and whispering endearments she wouldn't understand. Assuring her the boys would be returned. That he knew she was scared. That he was scared.

His hand travelled over her hair and his mind seemed to narrow its focus, the room faded until only the sheen of silk beneath his fingers existed. Rhythmically he stroked as he murmured until suddenly he began to speak more easily.

In his own language, not hers. All the things he'd bottled up for years but never said.

He said he knew how scared she was. How

scared one could be in that moment of loss. He could taste his first moment of absolute fear and horror, all those years ago on the ocean, at fourteen, not yet a man but about to become one.

The storm upon them before his father realised, the sudden wave that washed he and his brother overboard, and his father throwing them the lifebuoy just as the boom smashed him and his mother into the water after them.

He'd grabbed Gianni's collar and heaved him against his chest so his head was out of the water. He could remember that frozen instant in time. Them all overboard, Gianni unconscious and only he with something to cling to. He couldn't let go of his brother and, screaming out against God, he'd watched his parents sink below the surface.

So alone in the Mediterranean under a black sky. It had grown darker as the night came;

Gianni awoke, and he'd had to tell him of their parents' fate.

Such fear and swamping grief as they'd bobbed in the dark, imagining sharks and trying not to move too much, chilled to the core, fingers locked to the rope of the buoy. Knowing they would die.

Their rescue had been an anticlimax. A fishing boat pulled them in. Then the week in hospital alone and grieving, with visits from lawyers and one old aunt and her change-of-life son who'd hated them both.

He'd vowed that day he would be strong. And he had been.

He'd married Maria as his parents had betrothed them, and finally they'd had Paulo. His heritage safe again.

Then Maria had died and Paulo had been almost taken. He'd realised his life could fall apart again any moment and he'd needed to see his brother, his only family.

He, who'd never spoke of anything that exposed his soul, poured it all out to Tammy. It eased the burden of guilt he carried to tell her how he felt, without the complication of her knowing. From somewhere within it was as if the walls he'd erected around his emotions began to crumble, walls he'd erected not just since Maria's death, but since that lost summer all those years ago when he'd felt he failed his parents. Walls that prevented him being touched by feelings that could flay him alive.

He continued to murmur into her hair as her softness lay against his chest. His native tongue disguising the compromise and giving freedom to express the beginning of something he hadn't admitted to himself as he held her warmth against his heart. Her healing warmth.

The way she touched his soul. He told the truth.

How sorry he was to have brought this on her. How the lure of her physical attraction for him had begun to change to a more complete absorption. How she made him feel alive as he hadn't felt for years, even if sometimes it was with impatience or frustration when she thwarted him.

How beautiful she was, how she'd captured his attention after their first dance at his brother's wedding, how he'd never felt that connection before with another woman, even his wife, and that made him feel even worse.

How these past few days he couldn't stay away, spent his mornings and afternoons dragging his thoughts away from her so he could concentrate on business—something he had never had trouble with before—when in fact he was waiting for the evening when he could call on her.

The lonely nights dreaming of her in her house a street away, staring out through the window all night so he could start the whole process again.

How he'd glimpsed the promise of what could have grown between them, but now that had changed. Had to change. Once the boys were returned he would sit on a plane and watch the ground fall away beneath him, knowing she was still in Australia. So she and Jack would be safe, apart from the danger that followed him.

Knowing the distance of miles would not be the only distance that grew between them every second. But he would. Because she would be safe. Her son would be safe. His life was too complicated for this, the ultimate complication, but he could never regret these past few days. And he would never forget her.

Tammy listened. Her head on his chest, the regular beat of his heart under her cheek as his liquid words flowed over her. Some words and phrases she didn't catch but most she did, like the honesty in his voice and the gist of his avowal. The sad acceptance of his promise brought tears to her eyes.

When she lifted her face to his, he saw the tears and softness in her eyes and he could no more stop himself from kissing the dampness away than he could stop himself drawing breath. Her arms came up around his neck and her face tilted until she lay suspended below him, mute appeal his undoing.

He stood with her in his arms, cradled against him, and strode to her room, a dim and disconnected haven from the reality which they both sought to escape.

To hide in each other, buffer the pain of their fears with the physical, the warmth and heat of each other's bodies. At the very least the release might let them sleep.

Tammy knew she would regret this. But there were so many huge regrets—this tiny one was nothing if it gave her some flight from the pain, and comfort to them both.

He lowered her feet to the floor until she stood next to him, beside the bed, eyes locked as slowly they peeled away each other's clothes, layer by layer, like the emotions Leon had peeled away for her, until she was as bare as him.

She stepped forward until her breasts brushed his chest and with a muffled groan he crushed her to him. And she knew it was her turn to comfort him. She needed to comfort someone because she couldn't comfort Jack. Her hands curved around his neck and she pulled him closer so she could wrap herself around him, and draw his pain into her. In some unexplained way it eased her own suffering as they stood locked together in a ball of consolation that slowly unravelled into something else.

It started with a kiss, a slow gathering of speed. Kissing Leon was like running beside the wolf she thought him, down an unexpectedly steep hill, barely able to keep her feet. The momentum grew and her heart shuddered and skipped as she was swept alongside the rush of Leon, the heat of his chest, his powerful hands, his eyes above her, burning fiercely down as he searched her face for consent.

She reached up and pulled his mouth to hers again and she could feel the need in her chest and belly and in the heart of her as he gathered her closer, stroked her, murmured soft endearments of wonder in Italian which deepened the mist of escape and made her want to melt into him even more.

His hands slid down her back, marvelling at the smoothness of her skin, curling around her bottom and lifting her until her weight was in his hands. When he lifted her higher she rose against his chest. She'd never felt so small and helpless, dominated yet so safe and protected. She ran her cheek against the bulge of his arms, savouring the tension of steel beneath her skin from this mountain of a man who made her feel like a feather, as effortlessly he carried her until she felt the wall behind her. Then the nudge of him against her belly.

In a moment of clarity that came from the coolness of the wall on her back, she told herself she shouldn't do this, didn't deserve to experience this man at this moment in this way, would not die if she didn't. But she didn't really believe it.

She did believe she'd always regret not taking the gift of solace they offered each other in their darkest hour. And soon he would be gone.

He stilled, as if sensing her thoughts, and when she looked again into the midnight of his eyes, she knew she could stop this. Her heart felt the tear of denial, the breath of resolution and the tiniest lift of her skin away from his but something inside her snapped. No. She needed this for her sanity because with that one millimetre of distance between them, the outside world pummelled her and the pain made her wrap her legs around his corded thighs, hook her ankles and implore him to save her.

Afterwards, they lay together on the bed, entwined, her head on his chest as he stroked her hair and, against her will, against any conviction she'd be able to, she fell into a dreamless sleep and rested.

Leon listened to the slowing of her breathing

and his arm tightened protectively around her. How would he forget this woman? What had happened between them was something he hadn't expected and he certainly hadn't foreseen the severity of the impact of their collision.

More barricades had tumbled under her hands, barriers he'd closely guarded and never planned to breach. He would regret this night and yet could not wish it undone. His eyes widened in the dark when he realised what else he'd done. Or not done.

His sins compounded. Not only had he not protected her son, he'd not protected her.

The flash of light on his silenced phone was muted by his shirt pocket on the floor but he saw it. He buried the enormity of that other problem for another time as he slipped his arm out from under her head. She snuggled back into him and he paused until her breathing resumed before he slid from the bed.

His brow creased as he read the message, then he gathered his clothes swiftly and left the room.

CHAPTER SEVEN

SHE was woken by ringing as he came back into the room. He leaned over and switched on the bed lamp before he reached for the phone beside the bed and gave it to her. 'Yes,' she listened, mouthed, 'the police' at him and then said, 'I understand.' She listened again and then nodded, her eyes closing with relief. He could read it in her face. She put the phone down. 'They're safe.'

He didn't tell her he'd known already. Just turned her into his body and hugged her. It was her he needed to hug and not just because of the boys. Crushed her into his chest and closed his eyes as if blotting out all the terrifying pictures his mind had been filled with before his bodyguards had rung him.

Tammy pulled back and her tear-streaked face looked up into his. Searched his eyes, searched his face. 'They wouldn't have made a mistake. Would they?'

He shook his head. 'They're on their way home now.' He didn't tell her there had been a gunfight. Between two groups. Coming on them his men had scooped the boys from the confusion, had been fortunate one unidentified man had thrown himself in front of the boys to save them and been badly wounded. They'd left the dead and dying where they were for the police. He didn't say his bodyguards wanted to know what enemies he had that they knew nothing of.

Perhaps it wasn't over yet. It was an unexpected nightmare he'd dragged her into and he would never forgive himself. How many people were after him in his life? But there was much he didn't understand.

She searched his face and pulled away a little. 'There's more, isn't there?'

How could she tell? 'The boys aren't hurt.'

Still she watched him. Closely. 'Your people?'

He shook his head. 'No.'

Her head lifted as if she could scent danger. 'Then something went wrong with the kidnappers. So it's not finished.'

He squeezed her shoulders tight beneath his hands. 'It will be finished.'

She moved out of his embrace and her narrowed eyes flicked over him and away. 'You can't promise that.'

'I promised the boys would be returned.'

She looked at him and slowly she nodded. 'You did.' He could feel the distance grow between them. Despite what had passed only an hour ago. Or perhaps because of it. He thought briefly of a subject they hadn't broached but she went on.

'And I trusted you. But I don't know if I could do that again with my son's life.' And there was more there than was spoken and they both knew.

He inclined his head. 'I understand.'

She moved to slide out of the bed and he laid his hand on her shoulder to stay her. 'There is another thing we must discuss.'

She wrinkled her forehead. 'Yes?'

'I did not protect you when we made love. What of those chances?'

She shook her head. 'I'm meticulous.'

'Then there is nothing else you need to worry about.'

'Or you,' she confirmed.

The Saturday night before they left was so much harder to have Leon in the house, Tammy reflected with a sigh, thanks to a moment of weakness.

When she'd finally held her son safe in her arms that morning, Jack had asked if Paulo and his dad could stay their last night with them. Of course she'd said yes. She understood Jack's need and would have given her son anything he desired in that moment, that precious, arm-filling, flesh-and-blood hug of her unharmed child.

Both boys hadn't wanted to be separated after their ordeal and the day had been spent quietly watching over them as they slept and feeding them when they were awake. Leon had spent hours with the police.

How could she say no? What could she say, that she needed as much space as she could get from Leon now that she knew the man? Knew him with a depth and intensity and physical knowledge that scared the living daylights out of her.

Had heard his deepest fears exposed, had wept for the young orphan, had seen a little of his growing feelings for her. During her darkest hour those things had immeasurably comforted. Now they would both pay the price and tonight was incredibly awkward. And on top of it all was the guilt that Leon didn't know she'd understood his words.

Then there were the secrets he held. Where had he been when she'd been woken by the phone? Certainly not beside her in a state of undress. Plus the fact that two quiet men were outside, somewhere watching over her house and the people inside. She felt as if her world was spinning out of her control. She, who prided herself on control.

Leon had been reluctant to confirm their presence, but she'd seen them leaning on the tree across the road, and another out the back against her father's fence. His bodyguards.

Again she thought of Vincente and his cronies and the secrets and murky dealings she'd learned more of each day, and it hardened her resolve to stay aloof from this other dark man. But she needed all that resolve to not seek the same comfort she knew she could lose herself in.

The boys were finally asleep for the night. She'd been in and checked on them so many times she was almost dizzy with it.

Leon circled her, wary of intruding on her space, wary of her, as he should be. She was afraid of herself, her thoughts, her dilemmas that loomed large in the emotionally fogged compartments in her brain.

He came closer until he stopped in front of her. Lifted his hand and brushed the hair out of her eyes.

She shrugged and shifted out of his reach because she knew how easily she could have thrown herself back into his arms and that was the last thing she wanted communicated to him.

For Leon it was confirmation that she didn't need him. She had her son back. He was just prolonging her embarrassment. He watched her turn away again and search the room for the peace she obviously hadn't found next to him. 'The boys are safe now,' he said.

'Are they?' She sighed. 'Really? I have to bow to your superior knowledge, there, don't I?'

It was his fault. Letting her guess it was all not finished. He laughed without humour. Still she didn't trust him. 'Why don't I believe you could bow before anyone?'

Her eyes pinned him. 'Well, what if these criminals do come back to hurt the boys?'

He ran his hand down her arm. His aim had been to gentle her but all he seemed to achieve was to reinforce her agitation and his own aching feeling of loss. In the past twenty-four hours he'd changed.

Making love with Tamara had changed him. Had cost him something he hadn't wanted to give, ever again. But now was not the time to rail at himself for something he'd had no control of. Later he would sift what could be salvaged from the wreckage. He said again, 'The boys are safe.'

'You don't know that.' She looked at him. 'You can't lie that you aren't frightened they'll come back for Paulo.'

He sighed and he fought the dark pictures away. The way he'd only just caught them last time, Paulo pale and almost lifeless in his arms, the panic at the airport. The sickness of dread. And now again, unexpectedly, in this far-off land, and the fact that no ransom had been demanded. 'But there was no reason to take Jack.'

'There wasn't yesterday.' Tammy shook her head. 'But now he knows what the men look like.'

He raked restless fingers through his hair. Nearly all the men had been caught. With one close to the end when last he'd heard. 'What if it was not Paulo they were after?'

She shook her head. 'I don't understand.'

Neither did he. 'Is there any reason somebody would want Jack?'

Her hand flew up as if to brush aside the idea. Vehemently. 'Of course not. They were after Paulo.'

He watched her, narrowed his eyes as he tried to understand the nuance he was missing. Something that didn't ring true, though she'd never given him cause to disbelieve her before.

It was hard to pinpoint his unease. 'My bodyguard was told they were delivering Jack.'

She shook her head. 'They made a mistake.'

He heard her words but this was what he couldn't understand. There had to be a connection. 'What about his father?'

She avoided his eyes. 'He's never seen his father.' He'd been in jail for all of Jack's life, but she didn't want to share that delightful pearl of information. She shook her head again. 'Jack knows I haven't seen or heard from his family since Ben moved me out of Sydney eight years ago. Before Jack was born. Jack's father was not someone I'm proud of falling in love with.' And I'm not making the same mistake twice.

Leon sat and pulled her down next to him. 'How old were you, Tammy?'

She stood again and walked away. She didn't want to talk about this now. When she had her back to him she answered, 'Does it matter?'

Leon persisted and she didn't understand why. 'Does anyone in this man's family know about Jack?'

She shook her head but she didn't even know that. She'd been pregnant, fifteen, with belly quietly bulging under the bulky clothes she'd worn. Her grandmother had panicked and her father had arrived. Thank goodness for the love of Misty and her dad. She was fairly sure Vincente was working himself up from a petty gangster and she would have been in the thick of it.

'I guess his mother knew I was pregnant because she worked for my grandmother, but whether or not she knew who the father was, I'm not sure. The whole world knew when I left.'

'So perhaps they could know?'

What was he getting at, digging through this old history? That horrible black trepidation was creeping over her again and she hated the feeling. Mistrusted it more than ever after yesterday.

She felt cold and she rubbed the goose flesh on her arms. It wasn't a cool night. 'This has nothing to do with the fact your son was kidnapped and mine was taken as well. Don't try and blame this on me. Our life was normal before you came.'

'I'm sorry.' He thrust his fingers deep through his hair. 'You're right. Unless he was Italian there can be no connection.'

Tammy's breath jammed in her throat and she hoped Leon didn't hear it stick. Another shiver ran through her as her heart slowed and then sped up twice as fast. She could feel her blood trickling coldly in her chest as she tossed that idea around like a hard lump of ice. No way.

Leon crossed to her. Her face gave away

the turmoil he'd caused. He was a fool and a thoughtless one. 'Forget I asked. Please, Tamara, forgive me.' And he could do little else but gently draw her into his arms and kiss her.

She was so soft beneath him. Her cheek like satin against his face, her hair fluid under his fingers in that way he would never forget. How could he cause her more distress? He stroked her arm. 'Come lie down with me. Just to hold you. Nothing else. Let me keep you warm.'

She wanted to. So badly. It was a great theory to just hug and wrap themselves around each other and drift off to sleep but she doubted it would end that way.

She shivered again. 'I am cold.'

Was it wrong to want to lie with this man? To experience the immersion in another human being, to feel the power of her inner woman that she'd only just discovered because he'd shown her? She wanted to lose herself in him, or perhaps truly find herself, and in doing so maybe gain some peace. Why did this man, a man leaving tomorrow, have to be the one who had shown her that? The only man she'd ever sought peace from. Why was that? Why did everything go so wrong?

She wrapped her arms across her chest and attempted humour. 'If you took me to bed I don't know if I could keep my hands off you.'

The worried crease across his brow jumped and the tiniest twinkle lit his eyes. 'Perhaps I could sacrifice myself to your needs. If that should happen I would forgive you. Medicinal purposes, of course.'

No. They couldn't. There was the chance of the boys wandering in. 'I don't think so.'

'I could stay on top of the bedclothes.'

'And how would you warm me, then?' Perhaps that would work. She was so tired and cold and miserable and the thought of leaving her troubles for him to mind while she rested was beyond tempting.

'I'll be out in a minute.' She dived into the bedroom and shut the door. She imagined his face when he saw her in her too-big, dark blue striped, flannelette pyjamas.

But when she returned he didn't comment. Just took her hand and led her to the bed. She doubted he wanted to risk her changing her mind and making him sleep in the den. When she stood before him he took both her hands and kissed them.

'Tonight will look after itself.'

Sometime in the night she awoke, her pyjamas strangling her. Her arm had little movement where she lay on the ungiving fabric and she felt trapped. Trapped and claustrophobic by the material and ripped off by the thought that tomorrow Leon would be gone. The bare skin of her feet had wormed between his legs and soaked in his heat and his hand had slipped between the buttons of her shirt and rested like a brand to cup her breast.

She lifted her free hand up to move his fingers but instead she stroked the back of his hand. He kissed her neck.

So he was awake also. *'Stai bene?'* Then, 'Are you okay?'

She almost said *sì*. 'I'm a little uncomfortable.'

'Your pyjamas?' She could hear the laughter in his voice and the sound was more precious than she expected.

'Yep.'

'I have a solution.'

'I'm sure you do.' The solution was delightful.

The next morning dawned clear and bright. Unlike her head. Tammy still felt fogged with the twists and turns of the past few days, let alone the disaster of sleeping with Leon again. Her face flamed in the privacy of the bathroom. Goodness knows how she was going to face the boys. At least Leon had been up and dressed before either boy had appeared.

Today they left for Italy. She was still telling herself his leaving was a good thing.

Emma and Gianni returned to Brisbane today from their honeymoon and Montana was also driving up with Dawn, taking Grace to meet up with her mother and new step-father, before they all flew out.

Leon had taken the boys to the shop while she showered, to buy bread rolls and cold meats for brunch, a last-minute attempt to create some normalcy from Paulo's trip to Australia. A family picnic by the lake before they left.

She'd told Jack they weren't seeing them off at the airport. It was the last thing Tammy wanted—a long, drawn-out goodbye in front of strangers or even to sit opposite Leon at a small café table and make small talk in front of their sons. The picnic would be hard enough but at least it was private.

Tammy was meeting them back in the kitchen in half an hour to make the hamper. When they'd gone she slipped next door in search of her father.

Ben was painting the bottom of his old rowboat down the long yard that backed onto the lake. No trip to the beach this weekend. The ghost gum towered into the sky and shaded the grassy knoll above the water where he worked. The boatshed was where her father came when he was stressed.

She'd spent months of lazy summer afternoons with Ben and Misty here, watching swans and ducks when Jack was a baby. She realised time, peaceful and trouble-free time, so different to now, had drifted by like the floating leaves from the overhanging trees.

'Hello, there, Tam.' Her father looked up with a smile and his piercing blue eyes narrowed at the strain in her face.

He wiped the excess paint off the paintbrush and balanced it carefully across the top of the open paint tin before he stood. 'How are you? How's Jack? What's happened was huge. Bigger than anything we've had to cope with before.' He came closer. 'You okay, honey?'

She watched one large drip of red paint slide down the end of the brush and fall onto the grass like a drop of blood. A spectre of foreboding. But she didn't have premonitions—that was Misty's way. She shivered. She was here for a reason. 'I'll be fine when Leon's gone and Jack's safe.' As if to convince herself?

Her father's dark brows, so like her own, raised in question. He slid an arm around her shoulders and drew her to sit beside him on the circular iron stool that ringed the trunk of the biggest gum.

'You think the two go together, do you? Leon and trouble?'

'Of course.' So quickly she could say that but still there was that tiny seed of doubt planted last night, an illogical but still possible seed that maybe the trouble had come from her.

She wasn't sure how to broach a subject everyone in her family had left alone for more than eight years.

'Do you remember when you came for me that last time at Grandma's?'

Ben's black brows rose in surprise. 'Of course.'

'Did you ever learn much about Jack's father?'

Ben's arm slid away and he straightened and gazed across the lake. 'Yes. A little.'

She wouldn't have been surprised if he'd said, 'No—nothing,' so the other answer made her curious. She couldn't read his face. 'What could you know? I didn't tell you much.'

Still he didn't look at her. 'I found out what I needed to. To be sure you were safe when I took you away. To be sure Jack was safe.'

She really didn't want to hear those words. *To be sure Jack was safe.* Her stomach plummeted as she watched his profile. 'I think Vincente was involved with the mob on a small scale.'

Ben winced. 'I believe he was. I spoke to his mother and he was betrothed to a woman in Italy so he was never going to marry you.'

'Do you think there is any reason they'd want Jack now?' She'd said it. Out loud because she needed her father to deny, say it was nonsense, because she couldn't say it to Leon, whom she needed to tell.

Ben looked away again and didn't meet her

eyes. Her stomach sank and she didn't want to think about the ramifications of that. He hesitated but then he said, 'Can't think of one.'

Tammy sighed with relief. 'Of course not.'

CHAPTER EIGHT

THE picnic had been Jack's idea. The boys kicked a soccer ball between them as they walked down to the water along the shaded path and every now and then Jack cupped his hands around his mouth and called, 'Coo-ee,' across the lake. Paulo would imitate him. The echoes bounced off the hills across the lake and rolled back over the water and Tammy could hear the boys giggle up ahead as they trickled the ball between them.

Somewhere to the right a kookaburra laughed at nothing in particular and she drew the moment in with the breath of freshly mown grass that drifted across the street. It was good to remember what normal felt like.

Not that it was normal to have a gorgeous Italian man by her side. 'The hamper not too heavy, Leon?' Tammy glanced across as they strode down the leaf-strewn path.

Leon swung the hamper as if it was filled with fluff and nonsense but Tammy knew it must have weighed a ton. 'It's fine.'

Like heck it was. She'd put cans of soft drink, a thermos of freshly brewed coffee, mountains of savoury mini quiches, cold sausage rolls and a full bottle of tomato sauce in with the meat and rolls. Small boys could eat man-size portions. Then there were the sweets on plates Misty had forced on her.

As she walked she kept glancing at his bulging biceps and, becoming more noticeable, the veins in Leon's right arm. She clamped her lips on the smile that wanted to spread across her face. She could tell there was a little strain adding up. He swapped to the other arm.

By the time they'd reached one of the picnic tables under the trees she could've put a drip in his veins with a garden hose. She waited for the sigh as he lifted the bag onto the table and wasn't disappointed. She had to laugh.

He slanted a glance at her. 'And what amuses you?'

'How useful a man's arm is when you need it.' She grinned down at the hamper. 'I'm afraid I loaded the food up. On my own I'd have put it in the car and driven it down.'

He smiled and said cryptically, 'It kept my hands busy.'

Just one little comment like that and a dragon unfurled inside her stomach. He could seduce her in an instant in an open park with children a few feet away. How did he do that?

When the soccer ball came out of nowhere and almost hit her in the head, it put paid to the dragon and she stumbled back. Leon's hand speared out to knock the ball away, then caught her arm to help her balance. He turned and raised his brows at the boys.

'Oops. Sorry, Mum.' There was a pause and then Jack added, 'Sorry, Mr Bonmarito.'

'Perhaps you could aim for those trees behind you,' Leon suggested mildly, but the boys immediately spun to face the other way.

'You're proving handy this morning.'

'*Sì.*' Very quietly, under his breath, she heard him add, 'And sometimes at night.'

Tammy fought the tide of colour away from her cheeks and just managed to keep it in check as she began to unpack the hamper. Change subject. 'What time do you meet Gianni and Emma at the airport?'

'Five. Our plane leaves at eight.' Leon reached across and took the heavy thermos and weighed it in his hand. He raised his brows at her. 'Could you not find a house brick to place in the bag as well?'

She grinned. He made her smile and she sneaked a look at his handsome profile as he gazed across the lake. She'd miss him. More than a little. She couldn't remember ever being so at ease with a man on one hand and so supersensitised on the other.

Leon reached in and stole a juicy prawn wrapped in lettuce and she offered the tiny plastic container with seafood sauce.

He smiled and dipped, then took his time raising it to his mouth, a teasing light in his dark eyes and she couldn't help but follow it. He was laughing at her but it was nice. She watched him indulgently as he closed his eyes in pleasure. But when he licked those glorious lips, capable of such heat and hunger, last night flooded back and she wished she'd just given him the sauce and run away.

'Your seafood is amazing.'

'Ah.' Brain dead. Wake up. 'Yes. I love it.' She replaced the lid on the sauce in such a hurry it splashed over her hand, but before she could wipe it clean he'd taken her wrist and brought it to his mouth. A long slow sip of sauce and she was undone. Her dragon breathed a spurt of fire as her belly unfurled and there was no hope of keeping the pink out of her face this time. She glanced hurriedly at the boys but they were running and whooping between the trees with the ball.

She rushed into speech. 'Misty's excelled herself in sweets. It's almost embarrassing.' She opened the folded cloth to offer the plates with plastic film displaying their contents. 'Let's see,' she garbled. 'Oh, Lamingtons.' Bite-size Lamingtons, chocolate eclairs oozing creamy custard, tiny swirls of meringue with tart lemon sauce in the middle. And another squat steel thermos jammed with homemade ice cream and some waffle cones to hold the ice cream which helped restore her sense of humour. With the crockery and the thermos she'd bet that weighed a ton too.

Leon wasn't seeing the food. He would miss her. His hands stretched in his pockets where he'd thrust them away from her. He wanted to pull her into his arms and lose himself and could feel the tension between them stretching. Perhaps he should kick the ball with the boys as a more useful outlet for unexpected action. 'Do you need help setting out the food?'

She shook her head. 'A bit of space would be great.'

He grinned to himself. 'Always so complimentary. It is fortunate my feelings cannot be hurt.'

'Or mine,' she retaliated, and he turned away with a shake of his head. She could be stubborn and blunt to the point of offence, but despite her efforts he could see through the independent facade she insisted on showing him. He had the impression it was he that brought out this harsher side of her and he acknowledged she had reason to distance him.

'Kick me the ball, Paulo,' he called, and the boys whooped as he joined their game. Fearlessly Jack attempted to tackle and when Leon sidestepped him Jack fell laughing to the ground.

Paulo swooped on his father while he was distracted and stole the ball and the three of them were bumping and pushing one another as they fought for possession. It was no surprise that soon they were all laughing and wrestling on the ground.

The immaculate Leon Bonmarito rolling in the grass with two grubby boys. It hurt too much to watch. This was what she couldn't give her son, though Ben had the same man-versus-man mentality that boys seemed to love. She didn't understand it but could see that Jack was delighted with the rough and tumble.

Leon looked and acted so big and tough and yet he was so good with the boys. She wished she'd been spared this memory. Jack was sent rolling away and Paulo dived on his father. She was sure someone would be hurt soon. Then it would all end in tears. The table was ready, almost groaning under the tablecloth full of ham and silverside rolls and the mountains of cold savouries she suddenly didn't have the stomach for.

She called to the boys. 'Come and eat.'

It took a minute for her voice to soak into the huddle on the ground but then they brushed themselves off and walked back towards her, all smiling and filthy. She pointed to the wipes she opened at the edge of the food.

'You can all wash your hands.'

'Yes, Mama,' Leon said as he shook his head at the spread. 'I think we need to put out a sign and invite people to share.'

She began to pour drinks. 'That happens. If you see anyone, wave them over.'

Leon believed her. This past week had shown him a town full of generosity and warmth and the concept of sharing was in every connection he made. He bit back the tinge of jealousy that wasn't worthy of him. His own life was different, and he wasn't able to function like this self-sufficient small town could. He had responsibilities, people depending on him and his family business to continue to grow to provide a service for those in need.

He was glad they had the chance today to do something normal. Though the taste of this magical interlude would no doubt come back to haunt in his and Paulo's emptily spacious apartment in Rome.

By the time they'd finished what they could, the boys were groaning and tottering back to their ball and Leon had subsided with a sigh onto the picnic rug.

'Had enough?' Tammy teased, and she looked over at him with satisfaction. When you don't know what to do with a man, you could always overfeed him.

Before she'd been foolish enough to sleep with him he'd taken up a huge portion of her day even when he wasn't there in person. Now, with so many memories in all dimensions, he would be everywhere.

Tonight he would be gone and the long nights ahead promised little rest at all. She was such a fool. But the opportunity for further foolishness was drawing to a close and when he invited her with a questioning look, she eased down beside him on the rug until their shoulders touched. She had no problem imagining more. Her ears heated with the need to tell him her secret.

Last night, in the dark, after he'd warmed her in a way she would never forget, he'd whispered again to her in his native tongue and the burden of her deceit had grown impossible.

He'd whispered softly how being able to hold her in his arms had been the only thing that had kept him sane while the boys were missing.

That his guilt for drawing her into this mess had been very hard and her forgiveness so precious.

How hard it would be to fit back into his life as he remembered the feel of her weight against his chest and how much he savoured the little time they'd had together and the gift she'd given him.

All soul-exposing statements he didn't know she understood.

Maybe it could have been different if he didn't live on the other side of the world. She could never leave the lake, take Jack from his grandparents, leave her friends and her work and, if she was honest, her independence, and just move in with Leon. Not that he'd asked her.

But she knew she'd be unable to go to Rome and not be in his arms again.

'Do you think you will come to Italy next month? For the maternity wing.' It was as if he'd read her mind without looking. He shifted his attention back to her and it was her turn to look out across the water.

The smile fell off her face. 'Perhaps.' No, she didn't think so.

He slid his finger beneath her chin and turned her face towards him. 'You do not seem too sure.'

She met his eyes. 'I'm not. I need to think

about the idea when my head isn't full of kidnappings and work crises and other—' she grimaced '—emotionally charged events I'm not sure what to think of.'

He nodded and let her chin go. 'I won't pressure you. Though I'd like to. Perhaps you will think about it. I know my new sister-in-law would be pleased.'

Bring in the big guns, why don't you, Tammy thought with a sigh. Emma would understand though.

She looked back across the lake so he couldn't read her eyes. 'We'll see.'

The boys returned and fell down beside them. She saw the glances they exchanged at the closeness between Leon and herself and she ached for their naiveté. She'd wondered if Jack would be wary of Leon but he seemed to accept that the big man had a place in his mother's attention. Maybe because he knew that place had come to an end?

In the few minutes they all lay there before packing up, the simple pleasures of the morning rolled over them. Even the boys were silent and peace stole over their blanket.

The blue sky through the leaves overhead hurt her eyes it was so bright—or that's what Tammy told herself, why her eyes stung—and small puffy clouds skittered and were reflected in the lake that stretched away through the trees.

It was a perfect day for their overseas visitors to see before they left. The thought bounced around like an echo in her head. That's what they were. Visitors. Tammy felt the emotion and the hopelessness of the dream overwhelm her.

She heard the sharply indrawn breath of Leon beside her, and turned to see a small brown bird poke an inquisitive head out of the bush across from them.

A lyrebird, his beady brown eyes unblinking, tilted his beak at Leon and then stepped fearlessly out into the open less than ten feet from where they lay. The boys froze and covered their mouths with their hands, their little chests almost bursting with suppressed excitement.

The lyrebird lifted his brown, curved tail until it stood behind him like a fan, then shivered and shifted his feathers, until the upright display was to his satisfaction.

Only then did he strut and pivot in a stately dance to show them his glory.

When he opened his mouth the unexpected sound poured out. 'Coo-ee.' The notes from the lyrebird soared across the lake and bounced back at them. Strong and sure and perfectly mimicked on the boys earlier. 'Coo-ee,' the lyrebird trilled again, and he stared at them all as if he'd just given them a very important message. Then his tail fell and with regal disregard for politeness he disappeared back into the bush.

Tammy felt the air ease from her lungs, and the collective sigh almost lifted the paper napkins into the air. Jack whispered, 'A lyrebird. Grandpa told me about them.'

'It copied our call.' Paulo, too, was whispering.

'That's what they do. They imitate noises,' Tammy said quietly. 'They can copy anything. Even a baby crying.' She felt like crying herself it had been so magical. She sighed and somehow the load seemed a little lighter. 'We'd better pack up.'

Leon stared at the bush, his mind strangely less cluttered by the past. But no doubt that was because the present had been so chaotic. The bird had looked at him, and of all the memories of this place he would take with him today, that bird, and these people spellbound by his dance and song, would remain with him.

It was time for the Bonmaritos to leave. They'd said goodbye to Ben and Misty and Louisa already.

The fierceness of Paulo's hug surprised Tammy, as did her own in return. The lump in her throat grew as she hugged him back.

Paulo's beautiful dark eyes, so like his father's, so serious and young, seemed dreadfully in need of a mother. Her heart ached for him, and for Jack, and the loss of what could have been.

She tried to imagine how this quiet young boy felt, all he'd gone through, even worse than Jack because he'd been taken twice. She hugged him again. Paulo had to feel nervous.

She stroked his shoulder. 'Your dad will mind you.'

'*Sì.*' He nodded, but the concern stayed in his eyes. 'And who will keep you and Jack safe?'

'We'll be fine, honey.' She hugged him for the last time. 'Have a good flight and look after Grace and Aunt Emma for me.'

'Until you come?' He searched her face. 'Jack wants to come.'

'We'll see.' She glanced across to Leon, who seemed just as embroiled as she, with Jack. 'I'll think about it.' Not on your life was she going anywhere near Leon Bonmarito. Hopefully by the time he came back to visit his brother she'd be over this infatuation that had rocked her nice tidy little world.

Jack returned to her side, looked at Paulo and shook hands and then threw shyness to the winds and hugged the other boy, who hugged him fiercely back.

'You guys got over your mutual dislike, I see,' she teased, and they broke apart, both pink-tinged in the neck.

'He's okay,' Jack said gruffly.

'Too rrright, mate,' Paulo said with a stiff upper lip and a fine attempt at Aussie slang. His accent rolled the *r*'s and made them all laugh.

Then Leon stood beside her. So big and darkly handsome…and so ready to leave.

'*Arrivederci,* Tamara.' His arms came around her for a brief hug and he kissed her in the Italian fashion on both cheeks. Nowhere near her mouth.

It was as if they both knew it would hurt too much. With his head against her hair she heard him say, '*Addio, amore mio.*'

Ciao, Leonardo, she whispered soundlessly into his shirt and then she stepped back. 'Safe trip.'

'Come,' Leon said to Paulo. 'You have forgotten nothing?' Paulo shook his head and Leon closed the boot on their luggage. They would leave the rental at the airport.

It was time. He lifted his hand in salute, no last chance for a kiss goodbye, Tammy thought with an ache she'd have to get used to, but surely it was better this way.

With Jack by her side she watched them drive away and as they walked back into the suddenly empty house, Tammy felt a gaping emptiness in her chest that made tears burn her eyes.

'I'm going to my room,' Jack said gruffly, and she nodded. She wanted to go to her room too, and crawl under the covers for the rest of the day, maybe the rest of the year.

Five minutes later Jack was back. 'We'll have to see them off now.' When her triumphant son reappeared, brandishing Paulo's backpack like a glorious trophy, she had a ridiculous urge to laugh out loud.

Then common sense stepped in. 'No, we don't. We can post it to him.'

Jack shook his head decisively. 'It's got everything in it. His MP3 player, his phone, diary—' he paused for effect '—his mother's photos.' Jack knew he had the winning hand. 'What if all that gets lost in the post?'

Tammy rubbed her forehead and ignored the stupid leap of excitement in her belly. She'd have to take it. They'd have to take it. Jack wins.

'Maybe we'll catch them. It's three hours to Brisbane and a real pain.' Not that she'd planned anything useful today except feeling sorry for herself.

Tammy grabbed her keys with a heart that was lighter than it should have been. This was not good. She'd have to go through the whole painful farewell routine again and this time she was bound to cry. But if she had to do that, she was darn sure she was at least getting that kiss. A real one. To hell with the consequences.

Her eyes narrowed for a moment on Jack. 'You and Paulo had better not have cooked this up between you. I won't be impressed if we catch them and Paulo's not surprised to see us.'

They didn't catch them and half an hour into the drive Tammy accepted it was a dumb idea to try. Once she thought a police car was following her and she slowed down even more. She wished she'd remembered to bring her phone so she could have called Emma.

The plane didn't leave for another five and a half hours so she wasn't worried about missing them. Leon was meeting Emma and Gianni at the International Departure gates at 5:00 p.m.

As was Montana with Grace. She had plenty of time. It was only one-thirty now.

By the time she took her parking ticket from the machine at Brisbane airport Tammy had reached a definite point of regret for her decision to come.

And they'd all, especially Leon, think her mad to chase across the country to give back a bag she could have posted. She could have sent it registered mail, for crying out loud. It was Jack's fault.

Her mood wasn't improved when she realised that she and Jack were in such a hurry they'd forgotten Paulo's bag in the car and they'd had to race back and get it.

Dragging her son through the terminal, she wished herself home until finally she spied the signs directing her to the departure lounge entry. And there, towering above the crowds, big and dark and brooding with his broad shoulders lovingly encased in his grey Italian suit, stood Leon. Her steps slowed and her hand tightened on Jack's as she came closer.

Leon turned, as if sensing her, and his eyes widened with surprise and a warmth that almost had her fan her face.

Jack eased his hand out of hers and ran across to Paulo brandishing the bag. The two boys hugged and Tammy and Leon looked back at each other with raised brows.

Her feet slowed but Leon stepped past the boys without a word and walked straight up to her. *'Ciao, bella.'* His head bent and he stared into her face as if still not sure that she was real.

Her cheeks warmed under his scrutiny. *'Ciao,* Leonardo,' she said. It was safe enough to echo, and of its own accord her hand lifted to brush his cheek. 'You didn't kiss me goodbye.'

His eyes darkened and roamed over her. '*Sì*. For good reason.'

'And what reason would that be?' Her belly kicked with the heat in his scrutiny and suddenly they weren't in a crowded airport. They were alone, in a mist of vision that narrowed to just Leon's face.

'I believe that's a dare.'

Wasn't that how they started? 'It's been done before.'

His head lowered further and just before his lips touched hers she heard him whisper, 'But not like this.'

She should have realised how dangerous it was to challenge this man. Or maybe she was very aware of the consequences. That was the glory of it. When he finally stepped back, the hard floor of the terminal seemed to sway beneath her feet and he kept one hand cupped beneath her elbow until she balanced again. Some kiss.

He lifted her chin with his finger. 'Why are you here?'

Still vague and dreamy she answered absently, 'Paulo forgot his bag.'

They both turned to the boys, forgotten in the heat of the moment, a few feet away only minutes ago, but the place they'd occupied stood vacant. Two older men moved with a leisurely intent to stand and chat there instead.

Leon craned his neck around the men, and frowned heavily. 'Now where have they gone?'

The boys were running. A vague and nebulous plan had formed in the few moments their parents had ignored them. What if they ran away? Together. Somewhere safe, of course, just long enough to miss the flight, and ensure their parents had more time together. More chance to stay longer in Lyrebird Lake for the Bonmaritos.

A family in front of them were heading for an arriving bus, pushing luggage and laughing, and the boys followed them and two older ladies onto the bus.

'What is Long-Stay Parking?' Paulo whispered as they sat unobtrusively behind the noisy family.

'Don't know, but sounds like a good place to sit while we wait for the plane to go,' Jack said.

The bus filled quickly with those returning from holidays and trips to their cars parked in the furthest part of the terminal. 'My father will be very angry,' Paulo whispered, regretting their daring already.

'So will Mum, but they'll get over it.' Jack's

voice wobbled only a little. 'It's for their own good.'

'What if we get lost?'

'You've got your mobile in the bag. We'll ring your dad. Which reminds me, you'd better turn it off now.' He looked at Paulo. 'In case he rings?'

Paulo paled and hastily dug in his bag. '*Sì.*' He flipped open the phone and held down the key until the screen changed. They sat there and stared as the light dimmed and disappeared. Both gulped.

The bus revved and moved off. The trip seemed to take a long, long time. When it pulled up, the jerk thrust them forward in their seats while all around them people stood and lifted bags and shifted in a line towards the exit and a huge area with rows of parked cars. In every big square of cars, a brick waiting room sat on edge of the bus line, to provide shelter in case of rain.

'We could sit in that shed,' Jack said, less sure of the brilliance of his plan now that they were there.

Paulo didn't say anything but he followed the other boy with his head down, his backpack bumping on his shoulder like the weight of the world.

Both boys' eyes lit up when they saw the snack vending machine in the corner of the waiting room. 'You got money?' Jack said.

'*Sì.*' Finally Paulo smiled.

'I can't believe this.' Tammy felt sick and frightened and most of all incredibly angry and disgusted with herself. And the man beside her.

Leon was reaching for his phone. A muscle jerked in his cheek and his mouth had thinned to a grim line. 'This, I think, is a trick thought up by your son.'

The possibility had crossed her mind. A bit like the suddenly found backpack of Paulo's. But she couldn't admit that. Surely Paulo had some say. 'Why does it have to be my son?'

Leon's hand tightened on the phone. 'Because mine is aware of consequences.'

Not true but she wasn't going to fight about it now. She was too scared to have lost Jack again. 'Where are your clever bodyguards? What if someone's taken them again?'

'One has left to organise our safe arrival and the other I gave leave for a few minutes. He approaches now.'

Leon launched into a flood of Italian and Tammy battled to keep up. It seemed the body-guard had gone to buy a drink and also not seen the boys disappear. So Leon wasn't discounting the chance of abduction. Tammy turned to the elderly men beside them. 'Excuse me. Have you seen two little boys, dark hair, about eight years old?'

One of the men shook his head and the other stroked his chin. 'I might have, actually. Did one have a backpack?'

'*Sì,*' Leon broke in. 'Did you see where they went?'

The gentleman lifted his hand and waved. 'Running towards the exit. I thought it strange but they caught up with a family and I assumed they were with them. I'm sorry.'

'Thank you. You've been very helpful.' Leon gestured to the bodyguard and the man jogged quickly towards the exit. He slanted a grim I-told-you-so glance at Tammy.

Tammy's head ached with the beginning of a tension headache. How could the boys have done this to them? They knew how frightened she'd been. She couldn't believe this was happening and all because they'd brought a stupid bag to the airport. When would she learn that this man was trouble? Where were Jack and Paulo?

Leon flipped open his phone again. Then he swore in Italian. Graphically.

'Don't swear,' she said—anger was the last thing she needed—and rubbed her face.

Leon blinked. '*Scusi*. Paulo has switched off his phone.' He narrowed his eyes at her. 'And how did you know I was swearing?'

Good grief. She didn't have time for this. She shrugged and avoided his eyes. 'I didn't really. It just sounded like swearing.'

His eyebrows raised but he said nothing more. 'I will try the washrooms. Perhaps you could check the shops.'

She nodded but the fear was forming a monster in her throat. 'And what if we can't find them?'

'Then we'll check with the police.'

* * *

The next hour was fraught with false leads, and small boys that for a moment made her heart leap, and then ache with growing fear. The police had faxed through the photos of the boys to airport security and the inspector in charge of the previous kidnapping was on his way.

Tammy slumped against a pole outside the terminal and searched out groups for small boys. 'I can't believe we've lost them again.'

Leon ran his hand through his hair and glanced at his watch. 'Nor I. There will be retribution for those responsible.' The underlying menace in his voice made Tammy shiver and for a second she almost hoped for Jack's sake that they'd been kidnapped.

Leon glanced at his watch again. 'I must meet the inspector and Gianni should also soon be at the departure gate. And Montana with

Grace. Do you wish to come with me or remain searching?'

What? And stay here by herself, imagining the worst? 'I'll come.'

When they returned to the terminal again only Emma and Gianni were there. Leon broke into a flood of Italian and when he said to his brother that no doubt it was a hoax dreamed up by Tammy's son, Tammy shot him a look of such pure dislike, he paused midsentence.

Leon held his hand up to his brother and turned to Tammy. Her heart thumped at his comprehension. He searched her face, took her arm above the elbow and steered her away from the others.

His grip was more than firm. 'You understood everything I said?' The question came in Italian.

'*Sì,*' she spat back.

He dropped her arm as if it was suddenly dirty. 'This we will discuss later.'

'Or not,' Tammy replied, and closed her eyes as he walked away. She felt like burying her head in her hands but it wouldn't help. He'd never forgive her. But it didn't matter. Nothing mattered. The boys were the important thing.

The inspector arrived accompanied by his constable. 'I do not think they have been taken by the same people.'

'Why are you so sure?' Tammy had to ask.

The inspector shrugged. 'We have all except one of the men responsible for the kidnapping in custody or in the morgue. It seems the shoot-out was between two warring Mafia gangs. They planned to hostage the one man's son for the location of stolen property.'

Leon's brow furrowed and his impatience with this diversion was plain. 'What has this to do with my son?'

'Nothing, I'm afraid.' The inspector scratched his ear. 'It's the other boy. Our informant believes Miss Moore's son was the illegitimate child of one Vincente Salvatore. Mr Salvatore was killed in the battle. It is believed he protected the boys with his life.'

Tammy felt the look of incredulity Leon shot at her and she shook her head. Vincente was dead. He'd saved the boys. She looked at Leon but he didn't hide his contempt for more lies. She hadn't known Vincente knew. How could she have known that Paulo's abduction had been mistaken identity? All this fear and danger her fault—for a hidden heist. And all the time she'd blamed Leon for the boy's danger. 'I'm sorry.'

'I wonder what else I do not know,' he said quietly in Italian, and she could tell he didn't care if she understood.

The inspector went on. 'There's still one man

at large so we will be keeping an eye out. Might be prudent to be careful, Miss Moore.'

The airport security chief arrived at that moment to join the inspector and Tammy turned still-stunned eyes on him. 'We've isolated the video coverage in the time frame the boys went missing. It seems there's a chance they boarded the long-stay car-park bus. We're waiting for a patrol car now so we can check that out.'

Leon's phone rang. He glanced at it with an arrested expression and closed his eyes with relief. 'Paulo?'

He paused as the boy spoke. *'Sì.'*

He looked at first Tammy and then the police inspector. 'We will come,' he said in English. 'Long-stay car park. It seems they have run out of money for the vending machine.'

'I'll go,' Tammy said quickly. 'My car's just outside.'

There was an awkward pause as they all looked at Leon. The security chief pulled a pad and pen from his pocket. 'Give me the registration and they'll let you through.' Tammy wrote down the number.

'I, too, will come.' Leon's tone brooked no argument and Tammy was too emotionally exhausted to care. It was her fault the boys had been kidnapped. Vincente's fault. The fact rotated in her mind like a clothes line in the wind. Around and around. Leon's words sank in. It was a wonder he'd travel with her but she guessed he'd handed his own car in. 'Feel free. What the hell.'

'Don't swear,' he mocked as they walked away together. She gave him the keys in the hope he wouldn't get out of the car when they first saw the boys. At least driving back to the terminal would give them some cooling-off period.

Leon glared down at her as they walked. 'So, all this time it is you who has placed my son in danger—not, as I thought, my imposition on you. You should have told me his father was a criminal. And Italian.'

She ignored the part she had no defence for. 'It was more than an imposition to almost lose the lives of two children,' she said wearily, 'and I had no idea that Vincente knew about Jack.' That wasn't strictly true. She'd *hoped* Vincente hadn't known about Jack.

'Is that the truth or more lies?' He didn't believe her. Couldn't say she blamed him.

She rubbed her aching temples. 'Nothing warned me the Salvatores, or their enemies, knew of my son's connection to their family. As far as I was aware, there was no connection.'

Leon strode forward more quickly when he spotted her car. She had to almost run to keep up. 'It is well there is still time to leave today because I find myself wanting to shake you for destroying my trust in you. That you speak my language.'

She wasn't happy being in the wrong either. 'I know. If it's any consolation I'm embarrassed I didn't let you know earlier. But the longer I left it, the harder it was to tell you.'

He speared a glance at her across the roof of her car. 'So I have told you what is in my heart, my most inner secrets, and you are the one to feel embarrassed? My sympathies.'

He came back to her side and opened her door, and his courtesy while he waited for her to get in was an insult.

His sarcasm flayed her and she could feel the tears she refused to let fall. Would this horrible day never end?

She'd witnessed his utter emotional devastation, and for a proud man who barely showed emotion normally, of course it must be mortifying. He'd never forgive her. 'I can only say I'm sorry. And that I wish I could have told you myself before you found out.'

It seemed she could look forward to years of distrust and dislike whenever he visited his brother in Lyrebird Lake. At least there was no decision now about visiting Rome.

It wouldn't matter how hard she tried to re-establish their mutual trust after this.

CHAPTER NINE

LEON drove with icy precision.

They followed the signs to the long-stay car park and the operator at the booth magically waved them on when their car appeared.

Two small and forlorn boys stood sheepishly outside the brick shelter, little white faces pointed to their shoes as Leon and Tammy pulled up beside them.

There was silence until Leon spoke very quietly. *'Arrivare,'* he said to his son. 'Get in,' he said to Jack. Then he glanced at Tammy. 'Or does your son understand Italian too?'

'No.' Tammy didn't offer anything else. The silence stretched and remained in the car until Leon reparked in the terminal car park.

They all heard his deep breath. 'I do not want to know whose idea this was—' his cold glance brushed them both '—but I wish you to appreciate how frightened and upset both Tamara and I were when we found you gone. This has been a difficult week for everyone and I would prefer if no further problems arise.' His voice remained low but every word made Tammy wince. 'Or there will be retribution.'

Paulo held back his tears. *'Sì, Padre. Mi dispiace.'* He looked at Tammy. 'I'm sorry.'

Jack sniffed and nodded, then he, too, took a deep breath. 'It was my idea, Mr Bonmarito. Not Paulo's. I'm sorry.'

'It is to your mother you owe an apology, Jack.'

She watched her baby struggle to hold back the tears. 'I'm sorry, Mum.' Tammy just wanted to hug him but she couldn't risk him thinking he could run away ever again. And if she was honest, she was a little nervous of Leon, in the mood he was in.

'Thank you, Jack. And Paulo.' She fought back her own tears. 'Let's just get you Bonmaritos on that plane.'

They all climbed out of the car and walked silently back towards the departure gate. Incredibly there was still time for boarding. Tammy was so emotionally punch-drunk she couldn't wait to make her own exit.

She saw Gianni and Emma up ahead and it was like a seeing a drink machine in the desert. They had Grace so Montana must have been gone. Emma, her best friend—a welcoming face, thank goodness, from a world she understood and felt comfortable in, a face from home. Her steps quickened and she threw herself into Emma's arms and hugged her fiercely.

Emma hugged her back. The loudspeaker called another flight and reminded them all that time was running out and they hadn't been through customs yet. Emma searched Tammy's face and then looked to Leon and gave her friend one last hug. She blinked back the tears and glanced at her husband before she took her daughter's hand and they moved through the departure gate into customs. One wave and then they were gone from sight.

Which left Tammy with the thundercloud, two subdued boys and a goodbye that never seemed to end.

'Say goodbye to Tammy,' Leon said quietly to his son, and perversely Tammy wished Leon had called her Tamara.

'Goodbye.' Paulo moved in against her as she held open her arms. She cradled his dark head against her chest and her heat ached for him. *'Ciao, Paulo. Hanno un buon volo.'* Have a good flight. She may as well tell everyone she could speak it if she wanted to. Now.

Paulo's eyes widened at her faultless Italian and then he smiled. A beautiful smile. *'Sì.'*

Leon took the insult on the chin. She was mocking him. It seemed she had always mocked him. He'd made a fool of himself with her deceit. Did she have no shame? How had he allowed himself to be fooled by her smile? And yet he was tempted to throw everything to the winds and demand to know if she cared for him a little. He bit the impulse stubbornly back. Did he have no pride? Did he want to lower himself again? He was a Bonmarito! 'Goodbye, Jack. Look after your mother.' He inclined his head and it should not have been so hard to brush past her and walk away. But it was.

Tammy watched Paulo follow his father, his eyes shadowed as he waved one last time to Jack and her. Then it was too hard to see because her eyes were full of tears. But still she

couldn't look away from the broad back that
finally disappeared through the gate.

He'd gone. Leon's gone. She'd tried to apologise in the car, but maybe she should have
tried again before he left. Of course she should
have. Should have thrown herself on his chest.
Should have made him see she hadn't meant to
continue the lie, but opportunities had slipped
away. And in those last few seconds, she'd
only alienated him more. With her pride. Lot
of good that would do her now.

The fact slapped her in the face. She loved
him. Loved Leon. And she should have told
him she loved him. At least then they would
have both been exposed. The fact stared her
mockingly in the face as she watched strangers
disappear into the void that had taken the only
man she should have fought for.

And she'd been too stubborn and too cow-
ardly to beg him to forgive her. Too proud to

share the same thoughts and emotions he'd shared with her more than once. She felt the tearing in her chest as she realised her loss. The tears welled thicker and her throat closed.

Jack tugged on her hand, then jerked hard, and she brushed her hand across her eyes and turned back to look. What was the boy doing now?

She looked again. A man with a barely hidden wicked-looking knife had taken Jack's other hand and was pulling him away from her. Again. They were trying to take her son again.

A red haze crossed her vision; all thought of self-defence she'd learned for years flew out the window in this recognition of danger and she raised her handbag like a club and rushed at him, threshing at his face and head until he let Jack go. She kept hitting him until something hot and yet chilling struck her chest.

People stopped and stared as Tammy blinked at the sudden heat in her chest and the last thing she heard was Jack's scream. She fell as the air seemed squeezed out of her lungs and a steel band tightened slowly and relentlessly across her chest. The world went dark.

Leon made it to the first checkpoint, clicked his pen to complete the departure form and suddenly a word leapt out. *Departure.* His hand stopped. His fingers refused to write a letter and he'd grabbed Paulo's hand and spun back towards the entry.

Making their way backwards through the crowd had taken agonising seconds and he prayed she hadn't gone far through the terminal. He didn't know what he was going to say but leaving without a kind word because of stupid, stubborn Italian pride would not happen. He'd made the gate just as Jack had been accosted.

His heart exploded in his torso as he'd pushed past people to where he could see Tammy flailing at the man. He saw it happen with a horror he would never forget, the awfulness of the knife, and seeing her eyes close as she fell.

He hit the man once, with a force that snapped the man's head back, and the knife flew into the air and then clattered to the ground. The assailant slid to the floor where he lay unmoving and for a few seconds Leon hoped he was dead. Then he fell to his knees beside Tammy and slid his hand to her neck to feel her pulse. 'Can you hear me? Stay with me, Tamara. You'll be okay.'

He found her pulse. It was there, beneath his fingers, rapid and thready, as the bright red blood poured from the wound in her chest. He pulled his handkerchief from his pocket and tried to staunch the flow, glancing around for help.

'She's alive,' he said to Jack, beside him, and then Paulo was there too. 'Look after Jack,' he said to his son, and white-faced Paulo nodded and put his arm around his friend as both boys looked on in horror.

A security guard arrived and Leon snapped orders at him. 'He's stabbed her. I'm a doctor. Call for an ambulance.' All the time his brain was screaming, *No, not Tamara. Not here. Not now. Not ever.* Wrenching his mind away from the unthinkable he clinically assessed her. With one hand he lifted her eyelids and no flicker of recognition eased his fear. 'Stay with me, Tamara,' he said again. He rechecked her pulse, still fast but it was her pallor and the unevenness of her breathing that terrified him.

Then he saw it in her throat. The sign of imminent death. The tracheal shift from internal pressure within her chest. The veins in her neck began to bulge as the pressure of one lung expanding from within its layers squeezed the air out of the underlying lung and crushed her heart.

Gianni and Emma arrived, pushing though people who crowded around them. 'Thank God.' Leon gestured from where he was crouched. 'He's stabbed her lung.'

Without a word, Gianni took over holding the wound as Leon rolled her gently to check there was no exit wound.

'Where are the paramedics? There is very little time to decompress her lung.'

Emma fell to her knees and put her arms around both boys. 'What happened?'

Leon spoke across Tammy's body. 'He stabbed her. An ambulance is on its way.'

Jack sobbed and Leon grasped his shoulder to give him strength. 'Move the boys away, please.'

The paramedics arrived and they all moved

back. Except Leon. 'I'm a doctor. Tension pneumothorax. It needs releasing. Now.'

The paramedics, young and a little unsure, gulped, looked at each other and nodded. With barely controlled haste they opened their kit and removed their largest cannula normally used for rapid infusion of intravenous fluids.

The paramedic wiped the area with a swab but his hand shook so that he dropped the swab. The bleeding sped up. He hesitated. The gauge looked huge and Leon could feel the sweat bead on his brow as her veins stood rigid from her neck. Come on, he thought.

Still they hesitated, perhaps unsure, and Gianni leaned across his brother. 'Here.' He pointed to the precise spot. 'Between the second and third intercostal space.' Of course his brother had dealt with this many times in rescue from flying debris and it was enough to galvanise Leon.

He ripped Tammy's shirt where the knife had gone in and her skin looked alabaster in the artificial light of the terminal, with a slash of sluggish blood. Her low-cut lacy bra was stained a garish red and he pulled it down further with one hand. Her collarbone lay round and fragile and he slid his finger along halfway, then down, one, two spaces between the ribs.

He glanced at her face, her beloved face, and she had the blue of death around her mouth. Leon snatched the cannula from the man and slid it with precision between her ribs and through Tammy's chest wall. The hiss of air escaping made him want to cry. He who never shed a tear could barely see.

Leon sat back and the paramedic, spurred on by Leon's decision, apologised for his slowness and hastened to remove the stylet so that only the thin plastic tube remained in her chest. 'Sorry. Never done it before, sir.'

His partner handed the tubing that would connect the indwelling catheter to the Heimlich valve that stopped the air from leaking back in and immediately the blueness began to recede from around her mouth.

Leon felt the weight ease in his chest. Slowly her chest began to rise and fall with inflation as the air between the layers in her lung escaped and allowed the tissue beneath to expand.

Her breathing became more rapid and the blueness faded more. 'We'll cannulate before we move her, sir.' The paramedic was all efficiency now and Leon winced for his love when they inserted the intravenous line in her arm. Seconds later the cardiac monitor assured them all her heart was beating fast but in a normal rhythm. A few more seconds and she was on the trolley and they were all moving swiftly towards the ambulance.

Still she didn't regain consciousness. Leon's fear escalated. 'How far to the hospital?'

'Brisbane Central. Five minutes, tops.'

'We'll follow and take the children with us in Tammy's car,' Emma said, and she clutched Tammy's bag so fiercely it was as if she was holding her friend's life in her hands. They peeled away with Grace and the boys.

By the time they had her settled in the ambulance, Tammy's pulse was still rapid but appeared stable.

Leon took her hand and leaned down near her ear so she could hear him over the sound of the siren. 'I'm here, Tamara. It's Leon. I need you to listen to me. Jack is fine. We're all fine. We need you to hang on.'

He didn't know what he was saying. He just knew he needed to make sure she could hear his voice. Unconsciously he switched to Italian and he didn't care that if she woke she would understand every word. He ached for her to do so.

'I love you, Tamara Moore. The thought of you dying right there, in front of me, will live with me for ever. Why did I think I could go and leave you when it is plain to see you need me around you all the time?' He smoothed the hair from her still-pale features. 'I adore you with all my heart, my love. I need you. You must get well and we will plan our life together. If you will have me.' He rested his face against her cheek and to hear her breath was all he needed to keep going.

They kept him from her in Emergency, but after beginning one tedious form he brushed them off and at his most imperious he cornered a doctor and gained entry to her side.

He oversaw them insert the underwater sealed drain that would keep her lung from collapsing again, and watched the colour return to her face with bags of blood they replaced.

He followed her to the intensive care unit and supervised her transfer into the bed. The only person he couldn't bully was the specialist nurse who stared him down and told him to step back.

'She's my patient. When she's stable you can have her back.' And to the surprise of the other medical staff he did back down. Because, he thought with a wry smile, how like his beloved Tamara she was.

When Tammy woke up, she saw him asleep in the chair pulled up to her bed. His dark hair was tousled, his five-o'clock shadow heavily marked around his strong jaw. He was a disgustingly handsome wreck of a man as his cheek rested on her bed. She'd done this to him.

'I've been meaning to tell you,' she whispered,

and the air stirred between them. He shifted in his chair and opened his eyes. The warmth that poured over her brought the heat to her cheeks. No one had ever looked at her like that. As if her presence had brightened his whole world. As if the sun had just risen with six words.

His hand tightened where it still held hers and he raised it slowly to his mouth and kissed her palm.

'Meaning to tell me what, *amore mio*?'

'That I speak Italian. Have done since I was a teenager.'

'So we discussed,' he said, but he was smiling. 'But now you have told me yourself and I am glad you can.'

She searched his face. 'What you said in the ambulance. Was it true?'

'You heard me, then?' Such love shone from his eyes she couldn't doubt him.

'I was trying to stay away from the light,' she only half teased.

He squeezed her hand and kissed it again. 'Nothing I have told you is not true.'

She closed her eyes and relaxed back into the pillow. 'In that case, yes, I will you marry you.'

'Sleep, my love. And when you wake I will ask you properly.'

CHAPTER TEN

LEON BONMARITO allowed the blessing to flow over him as the priest joined him and Tamara Delilah Moore in holy matrimony. His heart filled with the joy he'd once avoided on his brother's face and he thanked God again for allowing him to find and keep his love.

He had no doubt that somewhere ethereal above them all his parents were smiling down at them.

The tiny family chapel on the hillside at Portofino, filled with the scent and delicacy of flowers, held smiling people most important to them both.

Their two sons, dressed again in their tuxedos, tried hard to contain their mischief in the front row with the flower girls but he had no doubt Tamara's parents would quieten them if they exploded.

His brother and his wife, her pregnancy just showing, stood at the altar as their attendants but could not keep their emotion-filled eyes off each other.

His housekeeper and her husband, who had served the Bonmarito family all of their lives cuddled up to Louisa, who had come for a holiday and to share their happiness.

There would be a party at Lyrebird Lake when they returned but this day, far away from the magic of the lake, was for them. To savour the solemnity of their vows and celebrate their love in front of a special few in a special place.

Afterwards, Leon took Tammy to honeymoon at the Hotel Macigno in Ravello. Their suite of rooms perched high above the cliffs where at night, when the boys were asleep, he showed her how much he truly adored her.

In the blue-skied days the boys flew kites under the watchful gaze of the nanny Leon had insisted on so they could relax, and the nanny was watched by Louisa.

As Leon and Tammy walked the cliff paths hand in hand, the spectacular Amalfi Coast shimmered below them and he pointed out traditional fishing villages and the reflected blue of the Mediterranean.

Nearby Amalfi, Positano, Capri and Pompeii beckoned for day trips and the boys flourished in the warmth of love that radiated from both parents as they played in the sea and explored the ruins of ancient cities.

Gradually Jack began to call Leon Dad, and though Tammy had told Paulo he could always call her Tammy, the boy asked, diffidently, if he could call her Mum. 'That is different to *Madre*, if that is okay?' And slowly their family melded, became one with a solidarity Leon thanked God for every day.

EPILOGUE

One year later

'WE DON'T have to go to hospital. You could call Misty and Emma and they could look after me here.'

'*Cara*, I would give you anything. But what is the use of following your every wish for the centre and then you choose to birth at our villa in Rome?'

Tammy shook her head stubbornly. 'I don't want to get out of this bath.'

Leon perched on the edge of the tub and regretted he'd made it so large. Large enough for two but not for two and the birth of his child. 'They will have the pool ready for you at the

centre. I promise. They're dying to have someone use it. You could be the first.'

'Misty and Emma have to be there.' She
sounded plaintive and he wanted to smooth
the worry lines from her face.

'Of course.' He'd agree to anything. He was
confused and anxious and totally bewildered
by the sudden change in his calm and level-
headed Tamara.

The boys were with Gianni and what had
begun as a slow romantic day before the birth
of their child had suddenly turned into a mutiny
he hadn't expected.

He smoothed the hair from her forehead.
'Come, *cara*, I will lift you out.'

She sighed and he watched her gorgeous
shoulders sink below the surface of the water
as if savouring the last pleasure to be had from
the day. 'I'm sorry, Leon.' She gazed up at him
and he saw the flicker of uncertainty in her

beautiful eyes. 'I think I had a panic attack when I realised today was the day.'

She reached for the handles at the edge of the bath and quickly he lent down to take her hand. She smiled with relief as she slipped her hand into his and prepared to climb out. 'Which is silly. Because I've done it before, and I know I'm designed to do this.' He didn't know if she was talking to herself or to him so he nodded encouragingly, trying not to pull her up so fast she'd realise how scared he was she'd change her mind.

She went on musingly now. 'But for a minute there I didn't want to admit that the time is here.'

She stood, her magnificent roundness running with water and bubbles and acres of shiny taut skin that made him bless the magic day he was allowed into her heart.

'You are such a beautiful Madonna with child,

my wife.' His words came out gruffly, filled with bursting pride and a smattering of fear for the unknown. He needed to have her and their baby safe and then all would be fine.

The drive to the hospital was accomplished with typical Italian chaos but, for once, traffic parted before the assertiveness of an extremely worried father.

Their journey from the front door to the birth room was faster than the speed of light so that Tammy felt quite giddy in the chair Leon had cajoled her into. 'Slow down, for goodness sake, before all my endorphins run for the hills.'

He slowed, just, and she chuckled to herself at this man, her husband, this anxious, gruff, darling man who was so unsure of the next few hours that his usual calm had been totally misplaced.

Her own moment of doubt was long gone. She knew all would be well. She knew her baby was waiting to meet them with the same anticipation she felt.

The ripples of conversation followed them. The Bonmarito baby was coming. No doubt there would be a hundred people in the waiting room when the boys arrived. It wasn't her problem. Her husband would sort that out.

They were through into the birth suite now. The eggshell blue of the rounded walls greeted her like a long-lost friend. She'd spent hours pouring over designs and new innovations to create the perfect birth space. No angles or corners, just soft and rounded curves and a welcome like a mother's arms.

The pool water lapped gently, waiting for her arrival, and against the large window overlooking the shifting branches of a huge tree outside, Misty and Emma also waited. Both women smiled in understanding at the harried look on Leon's face when he came to a halt in front of them. He looked down at his precious cargo and began to smile sheepishly. 'I may have panicked for a moment there.'

'For only a moment,' his wife murmured with a smile as she lifted herself out of the chair and was embraced first by Misty and then by Emma. She glanced at Leon. 'Perhaps you could ask someone to take the chair away, darling, while I get organised.'

Leon nodded and hurried away. The three women laughed softly until Tammy began to sway as the contraction built and they stood holding her as she leaned against them. She breathed in deeply, her belly pushed low with the breath in her lungs, and then a downward out breath full of power and rightness.

Misty held the Doppler and they listened to the steady clopping of Tammy's baby's heartbeat as the contraction faded away and was gone. Then a quick rest back on the couch while Misty ran her gentle hands over the smooth mountain of Tammy's stomach, finding the baby's head well fixed deep in the pelvis, baby's back to the right and all as it should be for the final descent.

'The bath, I think,' said Misty.

Tammy nodded and her loose sarong fell to the floor with her underwear. Before they could move, the next pain was upon her and her two attendants smiled at each other and glanced at the door.

'I want Leon.' Barely had the words left her mouth and he was there. Kicking off his shoes and snatching at socks, shedding his trousers and plucking off his shirt until his powerful shoulders rippled freely as he leaned down and lifted her back against him for a moment before he stepped easily into the bath with Tammy safe in his arms. 'I am here, my love. Lean back against me.' And they sank into the water.

Tammy lay back against her man, safe and secure, surrounded by the warm cradle of buoyancy and her husband's arms. The bath gave the ease of movement she hadn't wanted to leave at home and the ability to move her cumbersome body to each new position with a gentle shift of her arm. As the next pain rolled over her she closed her eyes and breathed. The water rose and fell and her belly heaved with the life of her baby within.

She knew Leon's arms held safe around them both. Her fellow midwives would watch over them all until the journey was complete, and her heart was calm.

When Tammy's baby entered the world she was born into the silence of warm water, the welcoming hands of her mother about her, and lifted gently to the surface to breathe her first breath under the awestruck eyes of her family.

Perfetto. Except her father was crying.

* * *

Paulo and Jack Bonmarito scowled at the visitors. The new Lyrebird Wing of the Bonmarito Cura Nella Maternitá postnatal wing in Rome was crowded with well-wishers and they couldn't get near the door to their new baby.

'It'll be a boy. For sure,' Jack muttered, and Paulo nodded glumly. With three boys the new one would have to be favourite but neither said that out loud.

The boys looked at each other and shrugged and searched for Leon in the crowd.

'Who are all these people?' Jack asked.

Paulo chewed his lip. 'Acquaintances of my father. Business partners, patients, relatives of people from our village.' He shrugged. 'They will go soon.'

'Jack?' Paulo tapped his shoulder to attract his stepbrother's attention. 'I do not understand how the baby is born.'

Jack looked at him. He had a hazy idea but

didn't really think about it. Or want to. 'Ever been to a farm? Seen animals give birth?'

Paulo nodded and then paled. 'You are serious? Who told you this?'

'Mum. That's what she did at Lyrebird Lake. What all the midwives do. Usually in the bath. People go there to have their babies. Mum catches 'em and cleans 'em up when they come out.'

Paulo had trouble getting his head around that. 'Does it hurt, do you think? For the woman?'

Jack shrugged and packed away the deep fear he'd been fighting with all morning. What if his mother died like Paulo's mother had? 'I've never heard a cat or dog complain. What about you?'

Paulo shook his head weakly. 'I feel sick.'

Jack grinned, suddenly glad his new brother shared his fear. It was amazing how much better he felt when he realised he wasn't the only one afraid. 'And you're going to be a doctor? Let's find Dad.' In the end it wasn't hard to find him because the door opened and their father towered over everyone else in the room.

Leon gestured to the boys and they pushed their way through. 'Come, boys. Come and meet your new sister.' Jack and Paulo looked at each other and a slow, incredulous smile mirrored on both faces. Jack fisted the air. 'Yes!'

Leon swept them in and they saw Tammy. Serene and smiling, sitting calmly in a recliner chair, not looking like she'd done much at all.

Jack sighed with relief. She was okay. Mum was okay. That hard lump in his throat was going away. Well, he guessed all she'd done was catch a baby of her own in the water.

Nestled in Tammy's arms, curled like a kitten, was a tiny, pink-faced baby, with dark, soft curls piled on her head. She had the softest, rounded arms and tiny starfish hands that fisted up to her chin and mouth.She blinked at them.

'Look at her eyes,' Jack whispered, and he peered over Tammy's arm at the baby and Isabella blinked as if desperate to focus on her new big brother.

Paulo nodded. 'And her fingers,' he whispered back. 'She's got tiny fingernails.'

And across their heads, Leon and Tammy exchanged loving smiles full of promise and pride and wonder at the blessings that surrounded them.

* * * * *